THE CALL OF THE CAT BASKET

A York Cat Crime Mystery

by

James Barrie

SEVERUS HOUSE
YORK, ENGLAND

This edition is published by Severus House

Typeset in Garamond 11.5/10

Cover illustration, frontispiece and end piece by the author
Graphic design by Burak Bakircioglu

ISBN 978-0-9956571-3-7

www.TheodoreCat.com

This book is dedicated to
Randolph and Stobart,
Who are both now napping in
The Great Cat Basket in the Sky

Theodore In dis-*Guy*-se

Contents

Basket Case 1

Milton Macavity 8

The Ice House 14

Street Cat Theodore 20

Utter Shambles! 29

Milton Gets a New Pair of Shoes 34

What Matters Most 42

Never More Than Ten Feet from a Rat 46

The Long Nap 49

Pussy's in the Well 55

Where There's Smoke 63

The Pub That Famously Floods 71

Battle of the Buskers 76

Sand Dogs 82

Oliver Bartholomew Relapses 88

Scenes from a Swiss-Yorkshire Restaurant 92

Death of a Dickman..99

Subterranean York 106

The Roman Bath 112

The Peacocks of the Museum Gardens 116

A Penny for the Percy 122

The Good Samaritan 125

The End of Purpleman 130

A York Ghost Story 136

Bovine vs Badger 141

Oliver Bartholomew's Last Drink 147

The Bonfire of the Macavities 151

Porridge Eaters 159

*'Buck did not read the newspapers, or he would have
known that trouble was brewing, not alone for himself,
but for every tide-water dog, strong of muscle and with
warm, long hair, from Puget Sound to San Diego.'*

Jack London, *The Call of the Wild*

Basket Case

Theodore did not read the newspapers, or he would have known that trouble was brewing, not alone for himself, but for every home-dwelling creature, fat or thin, hairy or furry, from New Earswick to Middlethorpe.

A protest march was planned for the city of York. Members of an anonymous anarchist group, who hid their faces behind Guy Fawkes masks, planned to descend on the city to protest about the government and the state of the nation. They were to be joined by several other groups: environmental protestors, students against fees, old people against death, cow welfare activists, badger cull protestors, members of a Radiohead Facebook group… You name it – they were descending on York in their thousands.

Theodore didn't like to think too much of the greater concerns of the human world, if he could help it. He was beyond caring. As long as he had food in his bowl and a warm place to sleep, he was perfectly happy. Happy to be unaware. If only humans took the same view, the world would be a better place. He yawned with sleepy satisfaction. Then something hit him on the head.

He opened his eyes and glared at the dirty nappy that was inches from his head. He sniffed the offending parcel. It smelled of human waste. Baby waste to be precise.

'Sorry, Theo,' Emily said, fastening the poppers on Joseph's babygrow. 'Didn't see you down there.'

Theodore looked up. Emily had just finished changing the baby, although Theodore preferred to refer to it as the Pink Hairless Interloper. He got to his paws and voiced his disapproval.

'Come on. It didn't hurt. We all have to poo, don't we now?'

Perhaps it's time you taught it to go outside, Theodore thought back.

Emily's attentions returned to the baby. 'You like tickles on the tummy,' she said, and Theodore heard the Pink Hairless Interloper giggle.

'You like that, don't you… don't you, Joey?'

And the Pink Hairless Interloper giggled again.

I think I'll go downstairs, Theodore thought. There might be more intelligent forms of life down there.

Unfortunately there was just Jonathan, who was staring blankly at the television in the kitchen, a mug of tea in his hand. He was watching the news, as if it mattered; as if what was going on in the wider world was actually going to affect his existence. Why couldn't I have had less ordinary humans? Theodore wondered.

Theodore padded past him and checked out the food bowl situation. His food had not been replenished since the night before. Even his water bowl did not have a cat's whisker of water in it.

He miaowed at his bowls.

'Shush,' Jonathan said, not looking away from the television. 'You'll get fed as soon as Emily comes down.'

Jonathan knew that cats don't miaow at other cats. Like human babies, they just use their undeveloped vocal cords to whine and bleat for food or drink from adult humans. They probably picked it up from human babies.

Theodore looked up at the television.

'In other news today,' the newsreader said, 'a cat has been found in a child's packed lunch bag on a roundabout in Tang Hall, York. A passer-by heard the cat's cries and came to its rescue. It is now being cared for by the York branch of the Cats Protection League.'

Theodore's ears flattened against his head. Best to stay indoors, Theodore thought, glancing at his cat flap. Bad things happen outside.

He looked over at his cat basket in the corner by the radiator. *Bad things happen outside*, the cat basket agreed. *As soon as you've had your breakfast, you come for a nice long nap. A good eight hour snooze will set you up nicely for the day.*

Theodore's internal monologue was interrupted by the television newsreader in the corner of the room.

'We have news just in… Milton Macavity, a convicted murderer, also known as 'The Napoleon of Crime,' is on the run from prison following a dramatic escape. Macavity was transferred to York Hospital early this morning, when it appears he faked an acute appendicitis.

'Before going into the theatre for an emergency operation, he overpowered two prison guards and assaulted several people, including hospital staff and members of the public, before leaving the hospital on foot, wearing only a surgical gown. The police have warned the public not to approach the ginger-haired man, but to phone them and report it immediately. He has a history of violent behaviour…'

'That's only a stone's throw away from us,' Jonathan said. He picked up his mug and had a drink of Yorkshire Gold ('a blend of 3 leaf origins from the top 10 tea gardens in the world'). 'An escaped convict in the neighbourhood… Whatever next?'

Whatever, Theodore thought. We should never have moved to Haxby Road. I think I might have said so at the time. Next?

He approached the cat flap and stared through the rectangle of clear plastic, as a precaution to exiting.

A clothes line was hung across the yard. On it there was a row of babygrows, bibs, tiny pairs of socks and then a mixture of Emily's and Jonathan's clothes. The air was damp and there was no breeze. Rather optimistic, thought Theodore.

Then a pink-faced man with short ginger hair and ginger stubble appeared. He was wearing only a hospital gown. It must be the escaped convict: Milton Macavity, Theodore deduced.

The man turned his back to the house, exposing a pair of dirty grey boxer shorts. He cast off the hospital gown and tossed it into the corner of the yard. He snatched a pair of black jeans from the line and began to put them on.

Theodore turned and miaowed that Milton Macavity, convicted murderer and escaped convict, was in the back yard stealing a pair of Jonathan's jeans.

Jonathan turned away from the television for a moment. 'You've got a cat flap,' he said. 'Use it.'

Theodore turned once more to the cat flap. Milton was now putting on Jonathan's red and black checked shirt. Theodore announced the latest development.

This time Jonathan didn't even turn round. He just said, 'I'm not going to get up and open the door. Just use the cat flap like any reasonable cat.'

Theodore looked back through the cat flap.

Milton was putting on a pair of light blue and dark blue hooped rugby socks.

Then came the voice from behind him. *Why would you want to go outside? You don't want to go chasing escaped convicts, now do you?*

Theodore turned round and looked back at his cat basket. It was positioned in front of the radiator. It was brown and furry with the roof stretching over to form a warm cocoon. One of Emily's old woollen jumpers lay in the bottom. Theodore had managed to knead the jumper to the point that she could wear it no longer and he had then inherited it. From the basket he could survey his food bowls, the cat flap and also any activity in the kitchen: the epicentre of the house. His cat basket was the perfect place.

Humans spend too much time looking for *perfect places*. Moving houses in the hope of happier lives. Expensive holidays in exotic locations. Retreats in remote wildernesses… They had yet to realise that the perfect place was a warm furry cave by a radiator. Life is oh-so-simple, if only you let it be.

Theodore blinked his eyes. He turned back to the cat flap.

Milton was wearing Jonathan's shirt, jeans and socks. The escaped convict looked down at his stockinged feet and the wet grass and shook his head. He didn't have any shoes, Theodore realised.

Then came the voice in his head again. *Just let it go*, it said. *They're just clothes. Who needs clothes after all? You come and have a sleep. This jumper is so soft. When you wake, everything will be just fine…*

Theodore knew he had to resist the call of the cat basket. There was an escaped convict in his yard, who had stolen half of Jonathan's wardrobe. He needed to take up the pursuit of this escaped convict. He nosed open the cat flap.

You don't want to go outside, came the voice again. *Bad things happen out there.*

Oh, be quiet, Theodore thought, silencing the voice in his head. He pushed his head and then his body through the rectangular opening. With a snap, the cat flap shut behind him.

Milton was standing just a few yards away. He spotted the big grey fluffy cat. He caught the cat's eye and placed a forefinger to his lips.

Theodore decided it would be wise to hold still his throat and not call out the alarm.

Milton walked over to the boundary wall. He jumped over it into the next yard.

Theodore padded over to where Milton had thrown the hospital gown. He sniffed it. It smelled of Old Spice deodorant and stale sweat. Theodore inhaled the odour, committing it to memory.

He glanced back at the house. From upstairs, he could hear the Pink Hairless Interloper squealing. From the kitchen he could hear the muted outpourings of the television. He miaowed at the house.

You know you don't want to leave the comforts of home, the cat basket called back. *Inside is good; outside is bad. Bad things happen out there…*

He looked at the side wall, over which Milton had vaulted. Then he looked back at his own house. He was going to have to go it alone.

His tail raised up behind him, Theodore set off after Milton. He jumped up on top of the boundary wall and looked across at the rows of backyards separated by red brick walls. Milton was nowhere to be seen.

Theodore sniffed the damp autumn air. There was the faint smell of smoke; the smell of used nappies in the outside bin, moulding leaves in gutters, car exhaust fumes and the scent of urine sprayed by a neighbouring cat. But he could not pick out Milton's smell and from that the direction which he had taken.

You can still come back, the cat basket called. *It's warm by the radiator. You can forget what you've seen. You can sleep away the day. You can dream beautiful dreams…*

And Theodore did consider giving in to the voice and returning to the furry cave by the radiator. *His perfect place.*

But then he heard voices. Raised voices…

Theodore jumped down into the next yard and then up onto the next wall, following the voices. He hurdled several boundary walls.

You really don't want to do that, came the voice, fainter now.

But Theodore's ears were pricked back and his tail was standing up straight. He was in hot pursuit. His next case had begun.

Milton Macavity

'Macavity's a Mystery Cat: he's called the Hidden Paw –
For he's the master criminal who can defy the law.'
T S Eliot, *Macavity – The Mystery Cat*

'Just hand over the trainers,' Milton said, 'and no one will get hurt.'

'No,' said the middle-aged man. 'Why should I?'

'Because if you don't I'm going to hit you.'

'No,' said the man. 'You wouldn't dare. I have high blood pressure…'

'I'm sorry about this,' Milton said.

Then he punched the man on the nose. The man's nose gushed blood down his shirt.

'Look what you've done,' the man said.

'You can't do that,' a teenage boy said. 'He's got high blood pressure.'

'I just did,' Milton said. 'Now, hand over the trainers.'

The man began to undo his trainers. He handed them over to Milton, who tried them on.

Theodore looked down on the scene from the garden wall. There were four people in the backyard: Milton, the middle-aged man with high blood pressure, his teenage son and a teenage girl, who was taller than her brother but shorter than her dad. A football was lying on the ground and a set of goal posts were painted in white paint on the back wall of the yard. Milton must have interrupted a knock-about, Theodore deduced.

Milton put on the man's shoes. 'They're too big,' he said. 'They're no good.'

'Can't you just leave now,' the man with the bleeding nose said.

'Not until I have some shoes,' Milton said. 'I can't go around without any shoes on now, can I?'

'Here, have mine,' the teenage boy said.

The boy took off his trainers and handed them to Milton.

Milton tried them on. 'These aren't any good. They're too small.'

'What about mine?' the teenage girl said.

Milton looked down at the girl's pink and white trainers.

'They're pink,' he said.

'Beggars can't be choosers,' the girl said.

'You calling me a beggar?' Milton said. He clenched his fists.

'I didn't mean it like that,' the girl said. 'It's just a saying.'

'Well, be careful what you go saying.'

'You want to try on my trainers or what?'

'Hand them over.'

When Milton had put the pink and white trainers on, he said, 'These fit just right.'

This is turning into quite a nursery story, thought Theodore from up on the wall.

'Can you go now?' the other man said, wiping blood from his face. 'You've got your shoes.'

'I can't just go,' Milton said.

'Why not?'

'Well, I'm an escaped convict. First thing you're going to do after I go is call the cops and spill the beans. Then they'll know where I am.'

They all paused as police sirens filled the air.

'An escaped convict?' the man with the bleeding nose said.

'That's right,' said Milton. 'Three hours ago I was in Full Sutton. I'm Milton Macavity, also known as the Napoleon of Crime…'

'I've never heard of you,' the man said.

'Why don't you lock us in the outbuilding?' the girl said.

'That's not a bad idea.'

'But we might be in there for hours,' the man protested. 'And I've got high blood pressure.'

'You shut up,' Milton said. 'Now get in there, the lot of you!'

The three of them walked into the outbuilding and Milton shut the door and then locked it. He tossed the key into an overgrown bit of garden.

The police sirens were louder and Theodore could hear the whir of a helicopter approaching.

Milton didn't hang about. He jumped over the goal posts on the back wall and ran off down the alley.

Theodore jumped down into the yard. No sound came from within the outbuilding. He trotted to the back of the house. He jumped up onto a windowsill. He looked inside.

A middle-aged woman was sitting on the sofa, reading a magazine. Theodore miaowed and dabbed at the glass. The woman got to her feet.

'Go away,' she said. 'I don't like cats.'

Why do I bother? Theodore wondered. Your husband has been assaulted and is now locked in the outbuilding with your two children while you sit and read magazines.

'I told you, I don't like cats. Stop miaowing at me and go away.'

She looked past Theodore and her eyes widened in alarm. She shook her head.

'Adrian?' she said. 'Sophie...William?'

A moment later she was out in the yard.

'Adrian!' she called, panic rising in her throat.

There was bashing on the door of the outbuilding and muffled cries from inside.

'Linda... We're locked inside,' Adrian shouted through the door.

'Where's the key?' Linda said. 'It's not in the lock.'

'He must have thrown it somewhere,' Adrian said, 'or taken it with him.'

Theodore miaowed from the flowerbed, where the key lay.

'Oh, shut up,' Linda shouted across at him.

'You what?' shouted Adrian. 'You telling us to shut up?'

'No, there's a cat,' Linda said. 'And it keeps miaowing at me.'

Theodore closed his eyes for a moment. Then he picked up the key in his mouth and dropped it onto a paving slab, so that it chimed out when it landed.

Linda turned round and spotted the key. She dashed over and grabbed it. 'I've found the key!' she shouted.

'Well, hurry up and let us out!'

Before Linda did, she turned her attention to Theodore. 'Scram!' she said and clapped her hands together.

That's all the thanks I get! Theodore turned and ran towards the back wall.

He jumped up onto the wall. He stared down the rain-washed alley. In the grey mist he could make out the Minster in the distance. There was no one in sight.

He's gone. You might as well come home now. There'll be biscuits in your bowl. And then you can have a nice long nap!

Before his cat basket could sat anymore, he jumped down and set off down the alley in pursuit of Milton Macavity.

'Where's Theo got to?' Emily said.

'He was about,' Jonathan said. 'He was miaowing at the cat flap earlier. He wanted me to get up and let him out.'

Emily looked at the backdoor. Overhead there was the whirring of a helicopter.

Jonathan said, 'Someone's escaped from prison. Milton Macavity. The Napoleon of Crime, they call him. He faked an appendicitis; then overpowered his prison guards at the hospital… He's on the run.'

'I've never heard of him.'

Emily passed the baby to Jonathan. 'Could you take Joseph while I feed Theo? His bowls are completely empty. No wonder he was miaowing. You know you could feed the cat rather than just sitting there watching television all morning.'

She filled his bowls and then opened the backdoor.

'Theo!' she called. 'Breakfast's ready.'

She looked out at the yard. Theodore was nowhere to be seen. A faint drizzle hung in the air. She called again for Theodore but still he didn't come. She looked at the washing line, thinking that the clothes would never dry in this weather. Then she realised that there were gaps on the line.

'That's strange,' she said. 'I'm sure there was more washing than that when I hung it out.'

'He killed somebody during a jewellery shop robbery,' Jonathan said, not looking away from the television. 'Ran them over. A hit and run…'

Emily glanced over at the television. The weather was now on. Grey clouds covered Yorkshire. It was typical autumn weather.

'Don't forget we're having lunch in town with my parents,' Emily said. 'Caesars, the Italian place. My mum swears by the saltimbocca in there.'

'I haven't forgotten,' Jonathan said.

Emily turned to face the backdoor. 'I'm surprised Theo hasn't come in for his breakfast.'

She took the box of cat biscuits and shook them.

'He'll come when he's hungry,' Jonathan said.

'But he's always hungry.'

Then Joseph began to cry.

'He'll want his porridge,' Emily said.

'They say he's very violent,' Jonathan said, holding baby Joseph to his chest and jigging him on his knee.

'Who?'

'Milton Macavity. The escaped convict…'

'I'm sure the police will soon catch him,' Emily said, and went to make some porridge for Joseph.

'Let's hope so,' Jonathan said. 'He could be anywhere by now.'

The Ice House

Near to Monk Bar and behind the beer garden of the Keystones public house, there is a small building that looks like a stone igloo and is known as the Ice House.

It was built in the early 1800s on the northern rampart of the city walls. Below the structure a hole was dug into the earth and in the hole ice was kept in warm months to stop it from melting.

These days it serves no purpose and is off the tourist trail. The entrance is covered by a metal grille that, until recently, had been padlocked. The padlock had been removed by homeless Oliver Bartholomew, who was using the Ice House as a makeshift shelter.

Unfortunately for Oliver, he was about to meet escaped convict Milton Macavity.

Theodore was standing in the remains of St Maurice's graveyard, a small grassed area with several gravestones, either standing erect or lying flush with ground.

He had managed to catch a whiff of Milton and follow him to this spot, but here at the junction in front of Monk Bar, the traffic fumes had obscured any trace of his quarry.

To his right there was an advertisement painted onto the gable end of a building. It announced in beige and brown:

Nightly, BILE BEANS, Keep You,
HEALTHY BRIGHT-EYED & SLIM

I don't think I'll be having any of those, thought Theodore. He looked back at the street in front of him.

He could give up the chase now, he reasoned. He had done his best. Maybe it was better to leave the police to get on with their work. He could find his way home and have breakfast. His stomach agreed that it was the best course of action.

Yes. You can come back now and forget all about your silly little adventure, came the call of the cat basket. *As if you could have caught this escaped criminal… You're delusional!*

With this last quip from the cat basket, Theodore narrowed his eyes. He was more determined than ever to track down Milton.

He scanned the pavements. He noticed several people in a group wearing plastic masks. The masks were of a man with a white face, moustache and pointed beard wearing a black hat. Two police officers were walking behind the group. As soon as the two police officers had passed beneath Monk Bar, Theodore spotted Milton.

The escaped convict in pink and white trainers and blue hooped socks dashed across the road and disappeared behind the public house on the corner.

If Theodore crossed this junction, he would be in unknown territory. The streets were filled with people. There were cyclists and motorists whizzing by in potentially deadly weapons. It was not a place for cats.

Another police car drove by, its siren blaring, its lights flashing.

He had a duty, he reminded himself. A duty to stop this thug from committing further atrocities. He blinked his eyes. Then he raced across the junction. Cars beeped their horns and braked to avoid the large grey cat.

Theodore made it to the public house. He went down the side of the building. There was a deserted beer garden.

Theodore looked at the side door of the pub. Had he gone into the building? But then he heard voices.

He looked over at the strange-looking stone building below the city walls. There were steps leading up to the Ice House. Theodore climbed up the steps. The voices grew louder.

The metal grate over the entrance was open. Theodore crept forward. There was a ladder leant against the wall, descending about ten feet into a dark pit.

'What else do you have in that bag?' he heard Milton say.

Theodore peered down into the dark.

He made out Milton standing over another man.

The second man was down-and-out Oliver Batholomew..

'Give me that knife,' Milton said.

'But I need it,' Oliver said. 'What am I supposed to eat with?'

Milton thumped Oliver on the head. Oliver fell to the floor. Milton grabbed up the canvas bag. He emptied its contents onto the floor of the Ice House. He stuck the knife in his pocket. Dozens of plastic bottles were strewn around the building. They had contained cider but now most of them contained urine.

Milton shook his head. 'This place is a right mess,' he said.

'I try to keep it tidy,' Oliver said.

'It's a disgrace,' Milton said. 'Now give me your coat.'

Oliver slowly took off his army coat. He handed it over to Milton.

Milton put on the coat. He looked down at his trainers and then at Oliver's army boots.

'And your boots…'

'Not my boots,' Oliver said.

'I'm sorry,' Milton said, 'but I need your boots. I can't go round in pink trainers. Whatever would people think? Me, an escaped convict. *The Napoleon of Crime* is what the papers call me…'

'You shouldn't worry so much about what others think of you,' said Oliver. 'You should learn to just be yourself.'

Milton clenched a fist and leant over Oliver, ready to strike him again. 'I'm having your boots,' he said. 'Whether you like it or not.'

'All right,' Oliver said. 'You can have my boots.'

He removed his boots and handed them to Milton.

Milton held the boots to his nose. 'They smell,' he said, 'like a slab of gorgonzola left in the sauna over summer in the Sahara.'

'I think I might have athletes foot,' Oliver said.

Outside there were more police car sirens.

'I can't wear them.' Milton threw the boots back at Oliver. 'Now get out of here!'

'But this is my home,' Oliver said.

'You're not supposed to be in here, are you?'

'Well, no,' Oliver said. 'No one should be in here.'

'I'm here now and you need to get out.'

He lifted Oliver up by his shirt. 'Now get up that ladder and clear off.'

Oliver slowly climbed the ladder. 'This is everything I have, down here,' he said.

'It's mine now,' Milton said. 'Push off and don't come back.'

Theodore caught the bearded man's gaze as he climbed up the ladder. His eyes were welling up with tears.

Theodore backed away and trotted down the steps away from the Ice House and back towards the pub, before Oliver emerged, blinking in the daylight.

Oliver followed Theodore into the beer garden. He sat on a bench and began to tie his bootlaces. His hair was overgrown and his face covered by a thick tangle of beard.

He spotted Theodore. 'Here, pussy cat!' he called.

Theodore kept his distance.

Oliver called again to him.

Theodore approached cautiously and then allowed Oliver to stroke him. He was just a homeless man who had been kicked out of his shelter, Theodore thought. The Ice House had been Oliver's special place, and now he had been kicked out of it by Milton.

Oliver picked him up and put him on his lap. Theodore rubbed up against him. I'm sure Milton will soon be on his way, he tried to reassure Oliver, purring against his new companion. Then you can have your special place back.

He looked across at the Ice House, in which Milton now hid. It was unlikely that the police would look in the stone igloo for the escaped convict. Not unless either he or Oliver alerted them. Maybe he couldn't apprehend Milton by himself, he thought, but now he had a human by his side, they might together bring him to justice.

He puzzled over how to alert the police to Milton's hideout while Oliver messed with his bootlace. He didn't realise that Oliver had removed the lace from the boot and formed a noose until it was around his neck. Oliver pulled on the end of the lace and it tightened.

Theodore protested loudly and tried to wriggle free but the waxed cord tightened around his neck.

'Now you be quiet, little cat,' Oliver said. 'We're going to be a team, you and I. We're going to make lots of money on the streets of York. Just you wait and see!'

I'm no Street Cat Bob, Theodore thought. I have a house and a family waiting for me. I have food in my bowls and a garden to use as a toilet. The street is no place for a cat. Especially not a cat of my pedigree.

'Yes, you're coming with me!' Oliver said. 'You're going to make me rich!'

He held Theodore up in front of him and laughed. His teeth were yellow; his gums were bloody; his breath was rancid.

Theodore closed his eyes and held his breath. I should never have left the safety of the kitchen, he thought. I should have stayed by the radiator and let the outside world carry on without me.

I told you so, came the knowing voice of the cat basket. *Now, see what trouble you've got yourself into... This is what happens when you don't listen to reason.*

Yours will be a life spent on the streets. A life of destitution and despair. It is a life of your own making.

Street Cat Theodore

'Every hour was filled with shock and surprise. He had been
suddenly jerked from the heart of civilization and flung into the
heart of things primordial.'
Jack London, *The Call of the Wild*

Monk Bar is one of the four historic gateways into
York. Today it houses the Richard III Museum.

On the pavement below Monk Bar, Theodore sat on
his haunches beside his new companion. Oliver had
placed several pieces of cardboard onto the ground to
sit on. At least there is something between me and the
cold wet ground, Theodore thought, trying to think of
a positive in the face of such adversity.

His new companion had swiped a pint glass from the
pub and placed it in front of them. In large letters on
the cardboard he had written:

MONEY FOR CAT FOOD
MUCH APPRECIATED.

The pint glass rang out every minute or so as people
tossed in their coins. More generous people popped in
fivers or tenners, which Oliver quickly retrieved and
stuffed into his trouser pockets. His plan to make
money by using the cat was definitely working. He
shivered in his damp shirt. As soon as he had raised a
decent stash, he would buy some cider to warm up.

Theodore had struggled at first to get away but the
bootlace around his neck that was tied around Oliver's
wrist tightened every time he pulled against it. In the

end he lay down on the soggy cardboard and feigned sleep. His brain, however, was more alive than ever. He needed to escape this terrible situation and deal with Milton before he could hurt or kill someone else.

While the escaped convict hid out in the Ice House, the people of York were safe. But Milton would get hungry before long and then come out. Prowling the streets of York. The next person he came across might not get off as lightly as the football-playing family or Oliver Bartholomew.

A girl's voice said, 'What's your cat's name?'

Theodore opened his eyes just enough to see a young girl standing in front of him.

'Smoky,' Oliver said. 'He's called Smoky.'

'Because he's grey?'

'That's right,' Oliver said.

'That's a rubbish name for a cat,' the girl said. 'Can I pet him?'

'It'll be a pound for a pet.'

The girl's mother rummaged in her handbag and produced a pound coin. She popped it into the pint glass.

Theodore allowed the girl to pat him on the head but he didn't purr. Smoky? What sort of a name was that?

Worst were the dogs. If they noticed Theodore, they would strain against their leads to get at the cat. Oliver had to pick him up several times and shield him from the excited canines.

And so it went on, for at least an hour. By which time the pint glass was half-full of coins and Oliver's pockets held half a dozen crumpled fivers and tenners.

'I think it's time for you and I to go shopping,' Oliver said.

He grabbed up Theodore in one arm and the pint glass in the other and made his way to a small supermarket on Goodramgate.

Several minutes later, he exited the supermarket, a plastic bag in one hand, Theodore in the other.

Emily and Jonathan were sitting in Caesars Italian restaurant with Emily's parents, Trish and Patrick. They had been seated in front of the large window, looking out onto Goodramgate. Emily and Jonathan on one side, facing the window; Trish and Patrick on the other, facing inside the restaurant. Baby Joseph was in a highchair at the head of the table, by Emily and Trish.

Emily looked out of the window and took in the street. She noticed a man walking by in a green army jacket. Probably some homeless guy, she thought. She noted that he was wearing the same red and black checked shirt that Jonathan had and also jeans that looked similar to Jonathan's and were too short for him. She looked across at Jonathan. He was wearing a dark denim jacket, some rock band T-shirt and beige cords. The cords were worn down at the knees.

'I think we should go to the Designer Outlet and get you some new clothes,' she said.

Jonathan glanced down. 'There's plenty of life in these yet,' he said, slapping his thighs where the corduroy was worn flat.

'I think I might have the saltimbocca,' Patrick said staring at the menu.

'Yes, you can always gauge an Italian by its saltimbocca,' Trish said. 'I think I'm going to have the same.'

'I fancy a Hawaiian,' Emily said, 'but it's not on the menu.'

'That's because this is an Italian restaurant,' Patrick said.

As everyone knows, the Hawaiian pizza is actually a Canadian invention. Along with paint rollers, peanut butter and Celine Dion, it ranks highly in the list of Canada's contribution to civilisation.

'I'll just have a margherita,' Emily said.

'I'm going to have a pepperoni,' Jonathan said.

'We need to order a bottle of wine,' Patrick said, his forefinger running down the wine list.

'Did you hear about the escaped convict,' Jonathan said. 'He escaped from York Hospital. Milton Macavity, he's called. He's supposed to be very dangerous…'

'Never heard of him,' Patrick said.

'Sounds like he should be on the stage,' Trish said, 'with a name like that!'

'They call him the Napoleon of Crime. He attacked a family on our street,' Jonathan went on. 'It was on the television just as we were leaving. They said that the police are looking for a man wearing pink trainers.'

'You'd've thought they'd be wearing more sensible footwear,' Patrick said and laughed at his own joke. Then, 'The merlot, I think.'

Trish tutted. 'That's not going to go with the saltimbocca.'

Patrick turned his attention to the whites.

Joseph scrunched up a napkin and threw it onto the floor and laughed.

Emily stared out of the plate glass window. Raindrops slid down the glass. The road outside was black with rain. People wearing Guy Fawkes masks passed; they all bore the same malevolent smile. A shudder passed through her.

'Those people in masks give me the creeps,' Emily said, still staring out of the window. 'I bet half of them don't even know he was born in York.'

'The only man to enter Parliament with honest intentions,' Patrick said, still studying the wine list.

'Excuse me?' Trish said.

'Guy Fawkes,' Patrick said. 'These postmodern anarchists have taken his image to demonstrate their own protest and anger at the government. They feel let down by politicians, who say one thing to get in, and when they do get in, do nothing but claim expenses.'

'Oh, rubbish,' Trish said. 'They just fancied a day out.'

'Maybe they have a point,' Jonathan said. 'Politicians aren't doing enough. If we don't start changing our ways, our children are not going to have a planet left. Man has altered the Earth to such a degree that in geology, we even have a new name for it: the Anthropocene Epoch...'

'Have you chosen a wine to go with the saltimbocca,' Trish said. 'Now where is the waiter?'

She understood that it was poor etiquette to bring up sex, politics or geology at the dinner table.

'Perhaps the chardonnay,' Patrick said.

The Holy Trinity is the only surviving church in York with box pews. The Victorians took a dislike to the old box pews and threw most of them out; they preferred people to sit in rows.

Within one of these box pews, Oliver made himself as comfortable as he could in his damp clothes and began to swig from a two-litre bottle of cider.

The partitioned-off room had been historically reserved for lepers. They would sit in the wooden enclosure, segregated from the rest of the congregation, and observe the service through a peephole in the screen.

'Not a bad start to our career,' Oliver said. 'What do you say, Smoky?'

Theodore voiced his opinion that any form of career was beneath him and he objected strongly to being called Smoky.

The back of Oliver's hand put a swift end to his protestations.

Theodore stared at Oliver's fingers. They were pink and swollen from the cold. They looked like big pink sausages. He took his chance and sunk his teeth into Oliver's fat forefinger. He held fast but Oliver's other hand grabbed him by the skin of the neck. He let go of the finger.

'You little blighter!' Oliver shouted.

He held the cat at arm's length in front of him.

Theodore struggled.

'Not so fast, little cat,' Oliver said. 'We're business partners, remember? You need to learn the ground rules.'

He grabbed at Theodore's collar. 'What do we have here then?'

He picked up Theodore's silver name tag that hung from his collar. The silver disc was engraved with his name and Emily's mobile number.

'Theodore, is it?'

Theodore tried to cry for help but no sound came out.

'Well, it's Smoky from now on.'

Then Oliver went to work with both hands. It took him some minutes to remove the cat's collar with his swollen fingers. He threw the collar as hard as he could across the church.

With his hands around Theodore's neck, he said, 'We are colleagues, you see? Me and you. A team...'

Theodore struggled once more to break free. It was hopeless he knew. He still had the bootlace around his neck that was tied to Oliver's wrist.

With the loss of his collar, he had taken another step away from his former life of safe domesticity. A few hours ago, he had been complaining about the tardiness of his food bowls being filled and dirty nappies being dropped on him from small heights. Now he had been stripped of his sole vestige of civilisation.

His collar told the world that he had owners, a home, a human family. Even if he managed to escape from Oliver and the life of the street, he wasn't sure that he could find his way home. *I should never have left the safety of the yard*, he thought, not for the first time that day. He let his body go limp.

There'll always be another cat to fill the basket, the voice in his head said. *You will be forgotten and replaced by a new kitten, who will appreciate me more than you did.*

He will not venture into town after escaped criminals. He will be content to stay by the radiator and wait patiently for his bowls to be filled. You will soon be forgotten. Emily will move on. We all know that the answer to departed cat is a new one.

Even Oliver noticed the change in Theodore's temper. He put the cat down on the wooden seat beside him.

'Oh, come on. It's not all that bad,' Oliver said. 'Life on the streets has its rewards. You'll see. We are free souls. Wanderers of the world. Free from the trappings of society. Unencumbered by mortgages, debts and taxes. We are free to come and go as we please…'

Well, I beg to disagree, Theodore thought, straining against the bootlace tight around his throat. *I was free before. Free to lie in my cat basket all day.*

Oliver took another swig of cider. 'You'll get used to it. You'll have to. You're with me now. We're a partnership, right?'

Theodore closed his eyes defiantly. I will never get used to this life. The street is no place for a respectable cat.

'I've even got you a little something.'

Oliver reached into his plastic bag and took out a pouch of cat food. He ripped it open along the top. He tried to tear down the side of the pouch but it wouldn't open out. He squeezed the pouch onto the wooden floor. Then he placed the cat on the floor facing the small mound of cat food.

'There you go, Smoky.'

Theodore sniffed the food. Carcass scrapings was his verdict. He turned his back to the brown heap of food, raised his tail high and let out a stream of urine. That's what I think of your cheap supermarket-brand food.

'You'll learn to eat what you're given,' Oliver snapped. He took a long swig of cider. 'You'll learn.'

After drinking two two-litre bottles of cider and half filling an empty one with urine, Oliver fell asleep and began snoring.

Theodore felt the bootlace slacken from around his neck. Now was his chance to escape. He tried to duck out of the noose but it got stuck around his head. He pulled against it but then Oliver snorted in his sleep and jerked on the bootlace. Theodore was dragged closer to the drunken Oliver.

He managed to place a paw across the bootlace so that it was held tight in front of his face. He began to chew against the waxen black thread, grinding it between his teeth. A minute later he had freed himself.

He darted into the corner of the box pew. He glanced back at his adversary.

Oliver jerked erect. He stared at the cat, his eyes yellowed and bloodshot. Seconds passed before he realised what was going on. Then he stumbled to his feet.

Theodore jumped up on top of a wooden partition.

Oliver lurched forward.

Theodore darted along the partition, narrowly avoiding Oliver's grasping hands.

Oliver fell to the floor.

Theodore navigated the wooden partitions of the box pews, making his way to the church entrance.

Oliver managed to get to his feet. He picked up a urine-filled bottle of cider and flung it at the cat.

Theodore jumped down onto the church floor as the bottle flew through the air. The bottle of amber fluid hit the stone wall behind him with a whack.

'You damned cat!' Oliver shouted.

And Theodore exited the church into the grey day and ran. His life spent begging on the streets of York was over.

Utter Shambles!

Oliver sat on a bench in the churchyard. It was raining steadily and his shirt was wet through. On the bench was a little brass plaque. It read:

> *'Benjamin Bartholomew*
> *Liked to Sit in this Churchyard.*
> *R.I.P.'*

From time to time Oliver Bartholomew glanced at the little brass plaque and took a gulp of cider.

'Daddy,' he said to himself, as there was no one else to hear him, 'I miss you.'

And he sat on the bench in the rain and cried to himself.

Kings Square was once home to a church, its yard used to keep flocks of animals before their slaughter by the butchers that were located in the Shambles. Blood flowed down the middle of this little street in medieval times. On this dull November day, blood would once more flow. But this time it would not be the blood of animals but human blood.

Theodore spotted Milton as he entered Kings Square from St Andrewgate. He had spotted the pink and white trainers Milton wore along with Jonathan's blue hooped socks. Otherwise he would not have realised it was him, as he was now wearing a Guy Fawkes mask like many people in the street.

Milton had snatched the Guy Fawkes mask from a table in the beer garden of the Keystones pub. He'd avoided the more popular streets, heading down Aldwark and then St Andrewgate, before he was faced with the crowd that thronged Kings Square.

An escapologist entertained the crowd. Many people had come for the protest march that evening, that had been dubbed the Million Mask March, but in the meantime they were playing tourist in the city. Milton was now one of the anonymous faces in the crowd, indistinguishable apart from his footwear.

As Milton made his way through the people he jostled a pair of Japanese tourists.

The woman said to her husband in Japanese, 'It's him… the escaped convict, Takeharu. Remember we saw on the news. They said he is wearing pink and white trainers, remember?'

'You're right, Yoshi,' Takeharu said. 'We must stop him.'

So the Japanese couple set off after Milton. They caught up with him in the Shambles. These days the butchers' shops have been replaced by Harry Potter shops with names like 'The Shop That Must Not Be Named'.

Takeharu placed a hand on Milton's shoulder. 'I know who you are,' he said to the masked face. 'You are the one the police are looking for. It is your trainers that give you away.'

Meanwhile Yoshi called the police on her mobile phone.

Milton turned to face the tourist. He was over a foot taller than him. 'Get out of my way,' he growled from behind his mask.

'No,' Takeharu said, 'you will wait here until the police arrive.' He placed a hand on Milton's shoulder. 'My wife is on the phone to them now.'

Milton glanced around. There were many people wearing the same mask that he had found discarded in the beer garden of Keystones. Some of these masked faces were now turning to him.

One of them said, 'Is that man bothering you?'

'Well, yes,' Milton said.

'You leave off him,' a masked man said.

'Excuse me?' Takeharu said.

'You leave him alone,' the masked man said. 'He's with us.'

'You don't understand.'

'Sod off, suit,' a masked woman said.

'You don't understand. This man must be arrested,' Takeharu protested.

'Who do you think you are?'

'I am a surgeon,' Takeharu said. 'A paediatrician.'

'What did he say?'

'I think he said he's a paedo.'

'A paedo? Let's have him!'

The masked woman pushed Takeharu. A man jostled him. He was surrounded by malevolent plastic faces. He fell to the ground. People piled on top of him. Then there was a punch to his head. Blood gushed from his nose. He raised his hands to protect his face.

The masked crowd kicked at his body. Some of them began to chant, 'One solution, revolution!'

Yoshi was pushed to the edge of the fray. 'Takeharu!' she screamed.

'Yoshi!' Takeharu gasped from beneath the scrum of masked protestors.

Theodore looked on from the windowsill of a shop. In the window there was a hand-written notice that read:

THIS WINDOWSILL IS OLDER THAN YOU.
PLEASE DO NOT SIT ON IT

I'm sure it doesn't mind, thought Theodore.

He watched as one of the masked men broke away from the melee and carried on down the Shambles, past the queue outside a Harry Potter shop. He was wearing pink and white trainers.

He looked on as Milton turned left at the end of the street and into St Crux Passage.

Takeharu had given up trying to protect himself. He lay slumped in the middle of the road. The crowd began to lose interest and parted around him. Yoshi ran to her husband's side.

Two mounted police officers entered the street from Pavement, their horses' hooves clipping the sandstone flags.

Theodore's gaze followed the mounted police officers, as they approached the Japanese couple. He noticed a street sign.

SHAMBLES, it read.

Yes, Theodore agreed: Utter Shambles!

He jumped down from the windowsill, skirting the queue of Harry Potter fans. He had no time for teenage wizardry. He set off again after Milton.

Back at Caesars Italian restaurant, Emily, Jonathan, Trish and Patrick were looking at the dessert menus.

'Isn't that Barbara from Scarborough over there,' Trish said, glancing at a woman at the next table.

Patrick looked up from his menu. 'I doubt it,' he said. 'I thought she'd moved to Market Harborough.'

'No, Trish said. 'You've got her mixed up with Shirley from Wortley.'

Just then Emily's mobile phone rang.

'I think I might have found your cat's collar,' a woman said.

'Where was it?' Emily said.

'In Holy Trinity Church,' the woman said.

'That's not far from us. We're on Goodramgate. Can you wait there? I'll be there in two minutes.'

'I don't have time, I'm afraid,' the woman explained. 'But I'll leave it on the altar, so you can find it.'

'OK,' Emily said. 'Thanks for letting me know.'

Once Emily had returned her phone to her coat pocket, Jonathan asked, 'What is it?'

'Somebody's found Theo's collar. It's in a church just off Goodramgate...'

'Theo must have followed us into town.'

Emily got to her feet. 'We need to go and look for him. He can't be far away... We need to find him.'

'But we haven't had dessert yet,' Patrick said.

'Dessert can wait till we get back to Acaster Mildew,' Trish said. 'Now you sort out the bill. We will go on ahead to Holy Trinity Church.'

Emily had already crossed to the pram, where Joseph was sleeping. Jonathan got to his feet too. A minute later they had set off to retrieve Theodore's collar and search for the missing cat, leaving Patrick by himself at the table waiting for their bill, the dessert menu still in front of him.

Milton Gets a New Pair of Shoes

Theodore stopped on the corner where the Shambles meets Pavement. Pavement is actually a street, so called because it was the first bit of road to be paved in York, back in 1378. Before then, it was known as Marketshire and was probably a bit muddy.

There was a small rectangle of grass adjacent to St Crux Church Hall. A low stone wall provided some protection against the passing hordes of humans. The top of the wall was studded with silver circles, where the former iron railings had been sawn off to be melted down as part of the war effort in the 1940s. However, most of the iron collected was not required, and the government of the day quietly disposed of the metal rather than admit it was more for propaganda than bullets to kill the enemy.

Theodore stood up on his back legs and peered over the wall. He scanned the passing people but saw no giveaway pink and white trainers.

You might as well give up the chase now, came the voice of the cat basket. *Cut your losses and come on home. Who knows what else might happen out there? Oliver might be out looking for you. And if you do manage to locate Milton, he will probably stamp on your tail and not give it a second thought.*

Behind the wall someone had left a half-eaten chicken burger even though there was a bin only yards away. He looked across the road and spied the Yummy Chicken shop from where the burger had originated. Behind the wall there was other human debris, mainly disposable coffee cups. Have you ever known a cat to litter? thought Theodore. We leave the world as we find it. If only humans behaved the same…

Theodore pawed at the grease-proof wrapper, exposing the remains of the chicken burger in a bread bun. He pawed away the bread. He noted that the chicken was smothered in white sauce.

Mayonnaise! If there is one thing Theodore could not stand, it was mayonnaise. Yummy Chicken! I don't think so, thought Theodore.

There are fresh biscuits waiting in your bowl, the cat basket said temptingly, *and fresh water in your bowl.*

Theodore blinked his eyes to rid his mind of the image of his food bowl. But his stomach growled insistently. He had not eaten all day. This was no time to be picky. He needed nourishment if he was going to continue the pursuit. Perhaps he had been a little quick to turn his tail up at the pouch offered by Oliver.

He took a bite from the burger and tried to chew without smelling. He gulped down the meat. This was not eating. This was survival. Survival on the streets of York. At this rate, he would be devouring mice, tails and all, by the end of the day.

With each mouthful of chicken, he realised he was moving further away from domesticity, further away from the comforts and boredoms of civilisation. He was stepping towards the life of the street. A life of constant danger. A primordial existence.

A man was sitting further along the wall. He wore a pin-striped suit and a pink shirt. The pin stripes of the suit were pink to match the shirt. The suit was crumpled and the shirt creased. There were flakes of dandruff on the shoulders of the jacket. The man had a dried smear of white on his stubbly chin. Mayonnaise, thought Theodore. It had to be the litter lout.

Theodore narrowed his eyes and folded back his ears.

The man had a bulky rucksack on his lap. He was bent over the rucksack, fiddling with something inside. His eyes were narrowed in concentration.

A young girl wearing a Guy Fawkes mask approached. She veered towards the suited man. As she got near to him, she spat on the ground.

The man looked up. Then he looked down at his shoes. Spit coated the toe of his right brogue. He looked at the girl who had spat on his shoe.

'What's your problem?' he shouted after her.

On the back of her black leather jacket were the words painted in white, 'CAPITALI$M $UCKS', and a portrait of Che Guevara. She did not turn round.

She may have a valid point, thought Theodore. We cats do all right without money. I have yet to see a cat carrying a purse.

Theodore's attention was drawn by a siren. He watched as an ambulance with flashing lights entered the Shambles. The ambulance slowed right down, as the Shambles is very narrow; the first floors overhang the footways on either side of the street. Pedestrians pushed themselves into doorways and through the alley into Shambles Market. The ambulance came to a stop halfway down the street, by the chapel dedicated to Margaret Clitheroe, who was a Catholic convert crushed to death below a door in 1586 for attending mass and hiding priests, later to be canonised in 1970.

Paramedics jumped out and rushed to the Japanese tourist's side.

In all the commotion, Theodore saw a pair of pink and white trainers dash across the street to the other side of Pavement, where they disappeared inside a shoe shop.

The shoe shop was located on the ground floor of Herbert House, a large black and white Tudor house that had once been home to a family of Herberts.

Theodore glanced at the remains of the chicken burger; then jumped down from behind the wall and set off after Milton.

'I need a new pair of shoes,' Milton said. 'These ones stand out too much.'

'Have you seen any you like?' the shop assistant asked, smiling. Her name badge read Becky.

'Well, I need some running shoes,' Milton said. He was on the run after all. 'Ones that don't stand out.'

'So not pink ones then?' Becky said, looking down at his footwear.

'Definitely not pink ones,' Milton said.

'Are you here for the protest?' Becky asked.

Milton realised he was still wearing the Guy Fawkes mask. 'I suppose I am,' he said.

'I was going to go down later,' Becky said. 'Once I've finished here.'

'Right, Milton said. 'Well, you be careful out there. It could get nasty.'

'I can look after myself,' Becky said and smiled. 'If you sit down over there, I'll bring you some shoes over to see if you like them.'

Milton sat down where Becky indicated. He took off his mask and put it on his lap. He removed the pink and white trainers and pushed them under his chair.

Becky returned with a trainer. 'Do you like this style?'

'Yes, they'll do,' Milton said. 'Just give them to me.'

'You need to try them on, don't you?' Becky said with a smile. 'Do you know what size you are?'

'Yes, a 10.'

'Well, I'll just go and get you a pair of size 10s to try on. I won't be long.'

Becky disappeared into the back of the shop, leaving Milton sitting on his chair. He turned his face away from the window and the world outside.

Theodore stared through the shop window. He noticed the sweat dripping from Milton's head. Police officers passed by but did not glance inside the shop.

Then he noticed a police van. It had stopped in front of the Golden Fleece further down Pavement. Two police officers got out and approached the shoe shop. Another police van pulled to a stop in front of Pizza Hut on the other side of Herbert House and two more police officers got out and approached.

Theodore looked through the window.

Milton was trying on the size 10 trainers.

'They're fine,' he said. 'I'll take them.'

'Do you want them in their box?'

'No, I'll wear them.'

'What's happened to the shoes you were wearing? The pink ones…'

'Don't worry about those.'

He stood up, pushed Becky aside and walked to the back of the shop.

'Hey! Where are you going? You need to pay for those.' Becky started after him.

Theodore looked to his left and then to his right. The police officers were still waiting to make their move.

There must be a back exit, thought Theodore. He padded in front of the shop and stopped in front of a passageway. It was sign-posted Lady Pecketts Yard. Theodore began to gallop down the passageway.

Ahead he heard a cry. He rounded a corner.

Milton had Becky up against a wall. She was crying.

Milton had a hand across her mouth. 'Look, I'm not going to hurt you,' he said.

Becky whimpered.

'You need to tell the police,' Milton said. 'Tell them there's a plot. Something big is going to go down tonight. They need to send for reinforcements.'

Then he let her go and ran off down the alleyway. As he turned right onto Fossgate, Theodore noticed the blue stripes of Jonathan's socks in the space between the bottom of his jeans and the top of his new black trainers. Milton must be quite a bit taller than Jonathan, Theodore deduced.

Then Becky screamed.

At Holy Trinity Church, Emily found Theodore's collar on the altar. She pushed the pram back to the entrance. She called her cat's name. He did not come.

'He's not in here,' she said.

'He could be anywhere,' Jonathan said.

Outside a firework went off with a loud bang.

'I keep forgetting it's Bonfire Night tonight,' Emily said.

'It's really not a night for a cat to be out,' Jonathan said.

'We need to find him.'

They exited the church. They began to search the graveyard. There was a sign tied to a tree that said, 'Phineas Bull'. Emily wondered who Phineas Bull was and why his name was on a sign tied to a tree. She heard a belch from behind her. She looked round and saw a man sitting on a bench, a bottle of cider between his legs.

She walked over to him. 'Have you seen a cat?'

Oliver stared at her with bloodshot eyes and belched. 'No. I haven't seen any cat,' he slurred.

She turned away from Oliver and called out for Theodore.

'Come on,' she said to Jonathan. 'Let's go this way.'

She pushed the pram towards Lund's Court, formerly Mad Alice Lane.

'I'd better wait here for your dad,' Trish called after them, 'or he won't know where to find us.'

Trish paced the church path. She wanted to get back home to watch *Gentleman Jack*, a BBC drama series about Anne Lister: a nineteenth century landowner, lesbian and diarist, whose union with her companion Ann Walker was sealed by taking the sacrament at Easter 1834 in the church in front of which she paced.

It was half an hour later when Patrick entered through the church gates, a redness to his cheeks and a sheen of perspiration to his brow.

'You took your time,' Trish snapped. She was sheltering from the rain in the entrance to the church by a large brass bell, which was engraved with the words: 'Ring for Peace'.

'I had to wait to pay, didn't I?'

'You had dessert, didn't you?'

Patrick looked guiltily at his wife. 'Well, I couldn't resist the tiramisu.'

'You can never resist the tiramisu!'

'Sorry.'

'I've been standing here for half an hour in the rain while you stuff your face with tiramisu.'

Patrick looked away, his cheeks reddening. 'Why isn't that Oliver Bartholomew over there?'

'Stop trying to change the subject,' Trish said but looked over at the forlorn figure on the bench. 'Young Oliver? It can't be.'

'I believe it is,' Patrick said.

He walked over to Oliver. 'Oliver? It's me... Pat.'

'Pat?'

'Yes. You remember? We were neighbours. I was friends with your dad…. Terrible what happened. A terrible business that…'

'Yes, Oliver said. 'Terrible…' and his voice faltered.

Patrick looked Oliver up and down. 'What on earth happened to you?'

'I suppose life has not treated me kindly,' Oliver said, defeat in his voice. 'Since dad had that… accident.'

Patrick sat down on the bench beside Oliver. 'I'm going to tell you a little story,' he said.

And then he told Oliver a little story.

What Matters Most

'Many years ago, I was down on my luck…

'Penniless… Homeless… Destitute…

'I had lost everything. One business after another had failed. I thought I would never recover. I was drinking. I was smoking. I was doing whatever drugs I could lay my hands on.

'I was sleeping in the doorway of an empty shop on Micklegate. I didn't even have a sleeping bag.

'One day a little old lady appeared.

"Here,' she said. 'I've made you some dinner. We can't have you going hungry when I've got food in the larder…"

'She handed over a large parcel wrapped in tinfoil. She then handed me a plastic spoon.

'I unwrapped the foil package. There was a whole Sunday roast dinner inside a giant Yorkshire pudding. No plate. Just a big Yorkshire pudding.

"I couldn't be giving away my crockery, now, could I?' the old lady said. 'So I put it all in the pud!"

'She then said, "Would you like salt and pepper? My husband would never eat owt without".

'And I said, yes, I would.

'So she put her hand in one coat pocket and took out a salt cellar and from her other pocket a pepper pot.

'After I used them, I handed them back and she popped them back in her pockets.

'I smiled my gratitude and the little old lady scuttled away.

'I looked down at the Yorkshire Pudding.

'Inside there were slices of roast beef, mashed potatoes, roast potatoes, peas, cauliflower, all covered in rich onion gravy. There was even a smear of horse radish.

'A whole Sunday roast dinner inside a giant Yorkshire pudding! Who would have thought it?

'I smiled to myself. And then I laughed.'

'Oh, get on with it,' Trish said. 'We're going to be here all day at this rate…'

Oliver stared at Patrick. 'Why did you laugh?'

'I laughed because I saw my way out of the hole I had dug,' Patrick said. 'That Yorkshire pudding gave me the seed of an idea.

'I managed to borrow some money. I went round all my old friends. I begged them. I said I would pay them back.

'Within six months, I had set up The Olde Yorkshire Pudding Shop. I took on the lease for the shop on Micklegate, the same shop whose doorway I had slept in for weeks. Every morning, as I stepped over the threshold I would remember my nights attempting to sleep in that doorway. I swore that I would never return to that life. I would make a success of this pudding business.

'By the end of that year, I had shops on every street that leads into this city. Micklegate, Fossgate, Goodramgate and Gillygate, and a flagship shop and restaurant on Coney Street.

'As you know, there are now Olde Yorkshire Pudding Shoppes in almost every town in this country. And I own them all!'

'You do?' Oliver said. 'I didn't know. I thought they'd always been around.'

'That's because I spelled Olde with an E on the end and Shoppe double P, E.'

'That was clever of you.'

Patrick waved a hand with a flourish. 'And you know what the bestseller is?'

'The Sunday Roast in a Giant Pud?'

'That's right,' Patrick said. 'The toad-in-the-hole is a close second though. But that's because I use only the finest Yorkshire sausages. And then there's the Full English Breakfast in a Pud. That's the bestseller before eleven o'clock. People come from all over the world to sample my puds…'

'Can you hurry this along?' Trish said. 'We do have a home to go to…'

'Well, that does bring me to the point I am trying to make. You see, it was all down to that little old lady giving me that meal in a Yorkshire pudding… One act of kindness and my life was turned around. And I said to myself that if ever I was in a position to help somebody turn their life around, then I would.'

'You would?'

'Yes, I would. You are coming home with us, Oliver Bartholomew. To Acaster Mildew.'

'He is?' Trish said.

'I am?' Oliver said.

'You are,' Patrick said.

'Well, he can stay in your den.'

'Yes,' Patrick said, 'you can stay in my den.'

'I can stay in your den?'

'Just till you get back on your feet.'

'Just till he gets back on his feet,' Trish said.

'I'd better get my things,' Oliver said.

Patrick slapped Oliver on his thigh. 'What matters most is how well you pick yourself up after you fall.'

Oliver nodded. His eyes had welled up with tears at this unexpected kindness.

Patrick got up from the bench.

'I think a hot bath is first on the agenda,' Trish said.

'I just need to get something,' Oliver said.

He got up and went inside the church.

'What a lot of codswallop,' Trish said. 'You've never been down and out in your life.'

'I said at the start that it was a story,' Patrick said and smiled.

They watched as Oliver returned. He carried a plastic bag containing a bottle of cider.

Patrick shook his head.

'What is it?' Oliver said.

'The deal is,' Patrick said, 'that you leave that bottle behind.'

'But it's almost full,' Oliver said.

'You leave it behind. You leave it behind with the rest of this sorry little chapter in your life.'

Oliver nodded.

'When we get back, we'll have a nice cup of tea,' Patrick said. 'I've got some Yorkshire Gold.'

'Yorkshire Gold?'

'They select teas from the top ten tea gardens in the world to make a rich, smooth and incredibly satisfying brew… A proper cup of tea, in other words.'

'Sounds good.'

'Well, let's get going,' Patrick said. 'A new chapter is about to begin!'

'It is?'

'If you want it to.'

Oliver nodded. 'I want it to.'

He put the bottle of cider down on the bench. Then he followed Patrick and Trish out of the churchyard.

A new chapter was about to begin.

Never More Than Ten Feet from a Rat

Theodore raced down Fossgate. The pavements were crowded and he soon lost sight of Milton. But then he picked up his scent: aftershave, sweaty socks and new trainers, the insoles of which had been sprayed in formaldehyde.

He passed over a bridge and stopped. The scent had gone. He turned and looked back the way he had come.

There were several police officers coming his way. One on a bicycle whizzed by. Two more on horses galloped down the middle of the street, the horses' hooves clacking against the cobbles.

Theodore began to retrace his steps until he picked up Milton's scent once more. He was standing next to the balustrade of the bridge. He stood on his hind legs and put his head through the balustrade. He looked down on the dark swirling waters of the Foss. Fifty yards downstream he saw Milton, wearing the Guy Fawkes mask, swimming silently away.

Police officers rushed by. He tried to stop them by calling out to them but they ignored him.

He looked down at the black water. He jumped up between the stone columns of the balustrade. Then he dropped into the Foss.

If you have ever tried to bath a cat, you will know that they don't like to get wet.

When Theodore surfaced, he coughed out a stream of grey water. He felt the cold currents pushing him along. He worked his legs. He was soon moving rapidly along the river, his ears folded back against his head.

Ahead of him he spied the Guy Fawkes mask that Milton wore. He was also being carried along by the flow.

On his right, he passed by York Castle Museum and then under another bridge. Ahead there was a crashing of water. He closed his eyes as he was carried over a sluice into the Foss Basin.

When he opened his eyes again, he saw boats tethered to moorings. He heard some splashing behind him. He turned and saw Milton swimming away from him.

He began to swim after him.

Patrick had parked his old Range Rover in St George's Field car park, parts of which abut the River Foss. He clicked open the car doors and told Oliver to get in the back. Then he spied something in the river.

'Well, look at that,' he said. 'There's a giant rat swimming in the Foss.'

Trish squinted. 'They say you're never more than ten feet away from a rat,' she said with a shudder.

'Yes. They do that.'

'Come on. Let's get going. The sooner we get back to Acaster Mildew the better.'

Trish got in the car and Oliver got in the back.

Patrick stared after the large grey rat. It was as though there was something familiar about it. Something he couldn't quite articulate.

'Hurry up and get in,' Trish shouted. 'And open the windows.'

Patrick shook his head. It would come to him, he thought. And if it didn't, it probably wasn't important. He burped and tasted tiramisu.

He got in the car and they set off back to Acaster Mildew.

Theodore was fast approaching Foss Dam. The dam's purpose is to stop water from the River Ouse backing up into the Foss and flooding properties upriver. Today the dam was not lowered and Theodore was carried straight through. He saw Milton pass under a little blue bridge ahead of him. Carried along by the strong currents he had no choice but to follow.

Two figures in black hoodies wearing Guy Fawkes masks looked down at him from the bridge as he approached. One of them pointed a finger at him. The other was holding a can of spray paint. He had just sprayed his tag on the side of the bridge in dripping red paint. At least when I leave my mark, there is little visible evidence, he thought, though olfactory evidence was another matter.

Then he met the black waters of the Ouse. He was dragged below the surface. He took in water. He was spun around. This would be his end. Drowned in the dirty Ouse.

His body would be washed ashore on some remote river bank, where his remains would be feasted on by vermin. Or carried out to the North Sea, where fish would nibble on his bloated corpse until there was no meat left and then his bones would descend to the sea floor where they would become one with it.

Everything became black. Everything became silent.

This was the end. The end of Theodore.

The Long Nap

Theodore was not the lightest of cats. Rather than being dragged down the Ouse by the currents, he descended through the water until he reached the sludgy bottom of the Ouse.

Among the near surface sediments, there was recent waste: shopping trolleys, rusted bicycles, bottles, cans, plastic debris and branches of trees brought downriver.

Further down he sank. There was an unexploded bomb dropped by a German bomber as it followed the Ouse back to the Humber Estuary in 1942.

Even further down and further into the past, there were watches, lighters, bottles, clay pipes, ceramic fragments, all dating from the early twentieth century.

Then, from the long reign of Queen Victoria, there came more bottles, jam jars and a ceramic doll thrown from a pram into the river by a spoilt Victorian child.

Images flashed through Theodore's mind as he sank deeper into the river sediments. He remembered the newsflash that morning, announcing the escape of convicted murderer Milton Macavity. He remembered being hit on the head by a dirty nappy just before he went downstairs to check on his food bowls. He remembered waking that morning.

Broken pipe fragments were all that marked the seventeenth century. Theodore sank back deeper into his own past.

He dropped through the air and landed on the woman's head. The woman screamed. She dropped the candlestick onto the floor with a clang. She roughly pulled him off her head and threw him to the floor.

Then the woman picked up the large candlestick she had dropped. Theodore ran into a corner of the church. He cowered behind the altar.

The woman held the candlestick in the air. 'You are going to regret ever setting eyes on me,' she said.

She held up the candlestick, ready to strike.

Theodore closed his eyes and tensed his body, waiting for the end.

He felt a warm liquid splash over him; it was not what he had expected death to be like.

He opened his eyes. Emily was standing in front of him, the other candlestick in her hands. She dropped it to the floor.

Ellen lay on the floor beside him. She was dead. He realised that the warm splash had been blood. Her blood. Emily had rescued him from Ellen.

That had been back in Acomb when Theodore had tracked down and brought murderer Ellen Black to justice. He had been a cat's whisker from death, Theodore thought, reflecting on this previous outing into bringing a criminal to justice. He had come close to having his brains splashed against the church walls. One of his nine lives spent.

Theodore sank further into the riverbed.

Passing through the medieval age, there were fragments of pottery: French jugs, German cups and mugs, Dutch cooking vessels; remnants of medieval York's trade links with Europe. There was a leg bone of a goose carved into a whistle. York at play was symbolised by dice and gaming pieces carved out of bone and jet.

Theodore passed further back into his own past.

He could see Emily and Jonathan crossing the road ahead. He waited until they had reached the footpath on the other side before approaching the kerb.

He didn't bother looking in each direction before stepping out into the road. His technique was to dash across as quickly as he could. So far his technique had served him well. He was alive, wasn't he?

Emily and Jonathan were walking along the footpath on the other side, further and further away from Theodore. He couldn't lose sight of them. He chose his moment and dashed into the middle of the road.

There was the screech of car brakes and the smell of burned rubber.

Theodore was lying flat against the tarmac. He opened his eyes. A little blue car had driven over him and come to a stop several yards ahead.

'Theodore!' he heard Emily cry.

She ran over and picked him up.

Theodore stared back into Emily's face, his eyes bulging, his heart thumping. He tried to wriggle free.

'I think he's all right,' Emily said, holding onto him tightly.

The door of the car swung open and a woman with short dark hair got out.

'Is that cat yours?' the woman asked, her voice high-pitched, verging on hysterical.

'He must have followed us,' Emily said, still clutching him.

'I could have killed him,' the other woman said.

Emily hugged Theodore to her chest, beginning to cry. 'I'm sorry,' she said.

'He gave me the fright of my life.'

'I'm sorry,' Emily said again.

Theodore tried to wriggle from Emily's grasp but she held onto him. 'You're not going anywhere, young man,' she said.

That had been another of his lives used up, Theodore realised.

He then began his descent through the sediments of Viking York. There were wooden cups, knife handles, combs carved from antlers, a leather shoe, wooden panpipes, beads and rings made from amber and jet, metal pins and fish hooks, a silver brooch, a handful of silver coins, some showing Thor's hammer or Odin's raven; others dedicated to St Peter, patron of York's cathedral. Theodore sank deeper, travelling further back into his own past.

He was trapped in a metal cage. The cage was in a darkened room, the curtains were never opened. He had been separated from his mother but still had some of his siblings for company. They were content to sleep most of the time, devour the food when placed in the corner and play among themselves. Theodore would stare out from the cage, between the thin metal bars. He wanted out. He knew there was more to life than this prison he was kept in.

Then one day the human came and carried the cage downstairs. There was a large dog in a cage at the foot of the stairs; Theodore's fur bristled. Then there was a room flooded with white light. The door to the cage was opened. Here was his chance.

He pushed past his siblings. He flung himself out into the world. Here I come! he thought, rolling across a soft carpet, before finding his paws. He heard the human's scolding voice. He began to run. In circles around the room, he ran. The door was closed so he carried on, circling the room. He didn't want to be put back in the cage. But there was no way out of this room.

After circling the room for some minutes he came to a panting halt. He lay on the carpet to get his breath back.

Then he heard a different voice. A different human.

'He's adorable,' a voice said. The voice was soft and kind.

He allowed the new human to approach him. He was ready to set off any second and begin his circling of the room again. But when a hand slipped beneath his stomach and another was placed on his back, he allowed the new human to pick him up.

'He's certainly a lively one,' the usual human said.

'Hello, little man,' the new human said.

Theodore pushed himself against this new human instinctively on hearing the voice.

'Can I take him home today?' the new human said.

Theodore looked up at her face. It was Emily's face. He purred with happiness. He knew he had found his human partner.

Where was Emily? Theodore wondered. She was the only one who could save him. Down and down he went. He had taken his last breath several seconds before. He sank deeper.

Roman times were represented in the muddy bottom of the Ouse by a silver denarius embossed with the head of Emperor Septimus Severus, a bronze helmet that had once belonged to a Roman legionnaire killed in a gladiatorial battle with a lion, a gold earring missing its partner, a fragment of an amphora bearing part of a human face. Then there were seeds and fruit stones: all that remained of the foods that had been brought from the Mediterranean to feed the Romans resident in Eboracum, their name for modern-day York.

Theodore sank deeper into the muddy bottom of the Ouse and further back into time. He was near the end of his journey. His thoughts were of his earliest memories.

He was beside his brothers and sisters, the siblings he would know only for a few weeks. They snuggled together against the warmth of their mother, vying for position against her furry body, trying to get at the soft nubs that gave them liquid life.

He felt a peace begin to consume him as he drank of his mother. He breathed in the scent of his family. A calmness transcended. Life was but a struggle. Peace was found in death.

He realised that this was not another one of his lost lives playing out in his head. He had returned to the beginning of his life, to the very start of his existence. It could only mean one thing. His life had come full circle.

Then came a familiar voice: *You should never have left me. You should have stayed at home where it was safe. Now you will visit the Great Cat Basket in the Sky. There can be no return from the heavenly bed. You will be watched over by Bastet. You will sleep the longest of naps. That's right: this is the Long Nap, from which there is no return. The Long Nap will give you the peace that you did not find in life.*

But before Theodore could give in entirely to the serenity of death and the voice of the cat basket, he was yanked upwards. Up through two thousand years of history.

Pussy's in the Well

A short distance beyond the Blue Bridge, there is a well, known as the Pikeing Well. Over the well, there is a building called the Well House.

The Pikeing Well and the Well House were built in the eighteenth century for promenaders along the then fashionable New Walk. The water was said to possess medicinal properties, so many would come and drink it and even wash their eyes with it.

It wasn't until 1929 that they realised that the water was poisonous and the Ministry of Health declared it unfit for human consumption. Following this announcement, the well was neglected and abandoned until its restoration in recent years. It was in this little building that Theodore came to.

He slowly felt his senses begin to return. He didn't know where he was. He only knew he was not in the river. He was not drowned. He had not ascended to the Great Cat Basket in the Sky.

There goes another life, Theodore thought. I really need to be more careful with them. He understood that Bastet can only allow nine lives per cat, which is plenty more than what humans are allowed.

Then he heard a voice.

'Ding, dong, dell,' it sang. 'Pussy's in the well.'

Theodore opened an eye.

'Who put her in?'

There was Milton Macavity squatting in front of him. 'Little Tommy Thin,' he sang.

His knees were pulled up below his chin.

'Who pulled her out?'

He stared past Theodore, at the stone wall that surrounded them.

'Little Johnny Stout.'

He was hugging himself to try to keep warm.

'What a naughty boy was that,' he sang in a broken voice, 'to drown the poor, poor pussy-cat…'

He twitched and blinked. 'Who never did him any harm… But killed the mice… in his father's barn.'

Milton jerked his head up, returning to the moment. He noticed that the cat had come to its senses. It backed away from him against the opposite wall of the Well House.

'I saved you, little pussy cat,' he said. 'You would've drowned if it weren't for me. I pulled you out. Are you not going to say thank you to your Johnny Stout?'

Milton's whole body was shaking from cold. At least he had found temporary shelter, in this old well.

In the debris on the floor of the well, he spied an old box of matches. There were also some cigarette ends. Kids, he thought.

He then remembered a short story his teacher had read to the class when he was at school.

It was set on the Yukon trail. A man walked alone to join his camp. It was so cold his spit crackled before it met the ground. Bad luck struck when his feet smashed through a skin of ice, into the freezing water below. If the man didn't light a fire, he would die.

So the man gathered twigs and moss and managed to light a fire using matches and a scrap of birch from his pocket. But he built the fire beneath the boughs of an overhanging spruce tree and his actions caused the snow to cascade from the boughs and the fire to be extinguished. The man desperately tried to light another fire, but his fingers were too numb, and he dropped his matches into the snow. He lost the ability to move his fingers but he managed to light the whole bunch of matches. Ultimately his final attempt at a fire failed. He ran along the trail on frozen feet in desperation. He collapsed into the snow. Finally he succumbed to the cold and died, out there in the vast snowy whiteness.

As the teacher read the story, it was as though the temperature in the classroom had dropped.

Milton felt a shiver run through him and the hairs on his bare arms stood erect. He looked out of the classroom window. It had begun to snow outside, and it was only the beginning of November.

Now, that's a writer, the young Milton had thought: a writer who could make it snow.

He couldn't remember the writer's name. Jack or John Somebody. Johnny Stout? No, that was something else. He glanced over at the sodden grey cat he had pulled from the Ouse.

He needed to get warm and dry out his clothes. He looked at the discarded box of matches. He glanced around the well house. There was dried moss on the walls, and twigs and leaves that had found their way in to this gated cave of stone.

'I'll light a fire,' he said. 'That'll keep us warm!'

He grinned at his companion.

Theodore agreed that it was a good idea with a raspy miaow of approval from his side of the well.

But what if Milton was planning on cooking him on a spit? If he had missed his morning porridge, he would be starving by now.

You're going to be barbequed, came the voice of the cat basket. *Roasted on a spit over a campfire. That's what comes of your getting involved in human affairs. You must learn to let them do what they do.*

Theodore looked outside. He heard fireworks in the distance. The skies were already beginning to darken. He got to his paws and made for the entrance of the Well House.

'Do you not want to get warm?'

Theodore turned. Milton had gathered up the materials with which to build a fire and placed them within a square hollow in the middle of the Well House.

Milton placed a lit match at the base of the fire and within seconds it had taken hold. 'Well, that was easier than in that story,' he said. 'We'll soon be nice and warm… And then, as soon as darkness falls, I'll be on my way. I'm on a bit of a mission, you see.'

Theodore looked at Milton with apprehension; then inched closer to the fire. He could feel its warmth on his fur. Through the flames, he eyed Milton cautiously.

Milton noticed his nervous stare. 'You got me wrong, little pussy cat,' he said. 'I'm not really a bad sort. The press made me out to be much worse than I am. All that Napoleon of Crime business…'

Theodore widened his eyes. *Oh, yes?*

'Well, inside it worked to my advantage. The other inmates kept their distance. I cultivated the image of a hard man so that the others would leave me alone. And it worked. You bite someone's ear off, they don't pick on you again.'

Theodore continued to stare at the convicted murderer.

'I'm not a bad sort really,' Milton said. 'I am just a victim of my environment.'

Theodore could understand that one's environment could affect one's behaviour and attitude to life. He had learned that from his few hours on the street.

'In prison, it was beat or be beaten,' Milton went on.

On the street, it was eat or be eaten, Theodore agreed with a slight nod of his head.

Milton removed his socks and shoes. He placed them close to the fire. He then removed Jonathan's black and red checked shirt, so that he wore only his prison-issue underpants. The pants were shapeless grey boxers, with the stains of a hundred other inmates of Full Sutton. Milton had never earned the privilege of wearing his own underpants while inside.

He then noticed a triangle of pink plastic poking out from beneath a heap of leaves.

'Now, what do we have here?' he said.

He picked up the pink corner and recovered a half-eaten bag of marshmallows.

'Well, that's a bit of luck,' he said with a grin. 'Must have been the kids, hiding goodies…'

He grabbed a twig, broke it into two and speared two marshmallows.

Theodore stared at the grinning pink man with ginger stubble on his head and chin, squatting over the camp fire in just his prison-issue underpants, toasting pink and white marshmallows. When I woke up this morning, I never expected this, he thought to himself.

'There you go!' Milton said, tossing a toasted marshmallow towards him.

Theodore sniffed at the toasted sugary offering. Marshmallows were not near the top of his list of favourite foods, but it was energy. Energy that he had expended while on the trail and energy that he would need before the day was done. He wolfed down the sugary snack.

Then he noticed the crescent moon of an appendix scar on Milton's lower abdomen. Milton followed the cat's stare.

'That's how I knew how to fake an appendicitis,' he said. 'Problem was, as soon as they saw the scar, they knew I had faked it. You only get one appendix, don't you? That's why I had to make a quick getaway from that hospital.'

Theodore narrowed his eyes. Probably not the greatest of criminal minds we are dealing with here…

'I should never have been put away in the first place,' Milton went on. 'I'm an innocent man.'

That's what they all say, Theodore thought, staring into the flames.

'The judge said it was "Joint Enterprise". That's what he called it.

'But I didn't intend to kill anyone. We just wanted his car. I wasn't even the one who was driving.

'He should have just let us take it, instead of trying to stop us. Who would have thought he would try jumping onto the bloody bonnet? It would have been insured…

'Well, I've cleaned up my act now. I got clean in prison. And I started studying a degree in law with the Open University… And I know I'm not guilty of murder. It was a robbery that went wrong. Manslaughter at the most. I didn't know he was going to try to stop us, did I?

'I didn't kill nobody.'

That's a double negative, Theodore thought; meaning you probably did.

Milton shook his head. 'That's the other thing about being inside,' he said and laughed. 'You end up talking to yourself!'

Theodore's mind was racing. All crime was the result of human weakness, he realised; human greed became human misery. Crime was the symptom of humanity. All humans were criminals… His mind was racing.

I must be having a sugar rush, he realised.

'He doesn't look the sort to shop in Urban Outfitters,' Jonathan said.

Emily looked over and saw the middle-aged paunchy man in a pin-striped suit with a rucksack on his back enter the clothes shop on High Ousegate, which describes itself as a 'hip retailer for apparel and home décor'. 'Maybe he wants a new look,' she said.

As she looked a teenage boy with long hair came out of the shop. He was wearing a black T-shirt that read, 'NON BINARY, in white capitals.'

'He'd be better off at M&S,' Jonathan said. 'People should dress their age…'

Emily's mobile phone beeped. She took it from her pocket. 'It's my dad,' she said. 'He never usually texts…'

'What's it say?'

'Just: "Might be worth checking the river. Theo might have fallen in".'

'The river? Is he drunk?'

'He can only just have got home,' Emily said. 'Maybe he has a hunch about Theodore.'

'Oh, come on. A hunch? You want us to go and search the River Ouse for your cat? He's probably back at home by now, on our bed or snuggled up in his basket…'

'Maybe,' Emily said. 'But I think we should split up. You go home and check if he's there and I'll keep looking in town. I might just have a walk down to the river. You never know. It's unlike my dad to have hunches.'

'What about Joseph?'

'He's going to have to stay with me, isn't he? He'll want a feed when he wakes up.'

'You're right,' Jonathan said. 'I'll head off back home.'

'Let me know if he's there,' Emily said. 'Or if he's not, for that matter.'

'Will do,' Jonathan said.

He noticed the worried expression in Emily's eyes. He gave her a hug. 'I'll see you soon,' he said. 'We will find him.'

'Yes,' Emily said. 'We *will* find him.'

Jonathan turned and began to walk the other way.

Emily put her mobile back in her pocket and pushed the pram past Fat Face, provider of 'casual clothing for an outdoor lifestyle' for people who don't like going outside very much.

Standing in front of her, there was a little man dressed as a fireman with lipstick marks stamped on his cheeks. He smiled at her as she pushed the pram past.

Ten minutes later, Miles Macavity exited Urban Outfitters.

Miles now wore a black corduroy Sherpa jacket and black jeans that he had only just managed to squeeze inside. On his feet he still had on his shiny black brogues. Over his shoulder he carried the large blue rucksack.

Next he went into Lakeland ('kitchenware chain with innovative gadgets and cooking utensils, plus homewares and garden products'), bought a knife with an eight inch blade and tucked it into the side pocket of his rucksack.

Where There's Smoke

Emily pushed the pram over the Blue Bridge, which connects St George's Field to New Walk at the confluence of the Ouse and the Foss rivers. There were two people wearing Guy Fawkes masks loitering in the middle of the bridge. It was late afternoon, the skies grey, overcast, the ground wet from the earlier rain.

Could Theodore really have ended up in the river?

She stared at the ground as she passed the two Guys on the bridge. Somebody had spray-painted 'Down with the system,' on the bridge's wooden deck in red paint.

Where did all this anger come from? Emily asked herself. The world's not perfect, she understood, but why were people so hostile to each other? It was like nobody could agree on anything anymore.

She stared at Joseph's innocent face, staring up at her from his pram. Noticing her gaze, he began to cry. His face turned a touch red and his eyebrows moved closer together.

Emily knew what it meant. He needed changing. Where am I supposed to change a baby round here? she wondered.

She pushed the pram onto New Walk and looked to her right at the river. The water was high. Branches and other debris sailed down on the water's dark surface.

Even if Theodore had somehow managed to get in the river, what were the chances that she would be able to spot him? Jonathan might have been right. Her dad had had two large glasses of wine with his lunch and probably another as soon as he got home.

Joseph's cries became more insistent.

'I know, I know,' Emily said.

But rather than turning round, she carried on, pushing the pram along the northern bank of the River Ouse.

She would find somewhere discreet where she could change Joseph. Then she would turn round and walk back to the city centre.

A firework went off in Rowntree Park on the opposite back. It screeched as it whizzed across the grey skies, bright green and then red. It exploded with a bang.

'You shut it!' Milton said, raising a warning hand at the cat. 'Don't you be giving us away now. Not after I saved you and then fed you marshmallows.'

Theodore had smelled Joseph. His nappy contents were like a fingerprint to his highly developed olfactory senses. Unfortunately the firework had masked his cry for help.

There were several repeated bangs from outside the well. Theodore's heart pounded in his chest. Bonfire Night was certainly not a night for a cat to be out. The smell of Joseph's nappy began to recede into the distance.

'If I get caught,' Milton said, 'a lot of people are going to get hurt. Something serious is going to go down tonight. That I am sure of. I'm the only one who can stop it.'

Theodore's eyes widened.

'It's my brother, Miles,' Milton went on. 'He's planning on doing something, something big. Bonfire Night's going to end with a bang. That's what he said.

I'm not a hundred percent sure what he's planning. But he told me that he was going to make a stand. Against the hypocrisy. Against the bullshit. Against the system that destroyed his career…

'That's why I had to get out of Full Sutton. They didn't believe me. The guards laughed at me when I tried to tell them. But I knew. You see, some spice head had had a mobile phone smuggled in… Flew it in by drone.

'I paid to borrow it. I phoned Miles and he told me. He knew I couldn't do anything about it. That just made him happier. "There's nothing you can do about it," he said, laughing down the phone at me.

'I knew I had to do something about it. You see, I'm not a bad guy. I've had my troubles. But I know right from wrong. Miles, on the other hand, is a deviant. He's malicious. What he has in mind could be anything. I know he means war though. War against the anti-establishment that destroyed his banking career.

'That's what he said to me. *This is war.* He's going to target the protest. The Million Mask March.'

Theodore stared into Milton's face. It was pink and stubbly. His eyes were ringed in grey. Was he telling the truth?

He's making it up, came the voice in his head. *And besides, even if his brother Miles was planning some terrible atrocity, do you really think that you could stop him? You're just a big fluffy cat!*

Outside the Well House, Theodore smelled Joseph returning, the smell still there but now only faint. She must have changed him, Theodore deduced. The nappy bagged and riding in the undercarriage of the pram.

He heard Emily call his name outside.

Just go to her and you'll be home in a matter of minutes. You could ride home with little Joey in the pram, nice and snug in there. You could have a nice snack of biscuits when you get in and then get warm by the radiator. I'm here waiting for you!

Theodore looked back into Milton's pink face. He made his decision.

There was truth in what Milton had told him. Why else would he have broken out of prison as he had and missed his breakfast? He would no doubt be caught sooner or later. He had broken out to stop his brother Miles committing whatever act of terror he was plotting.

Emily pushed the pram back along New Walk towards the Blue Bridge. She had managed to find a secluded spot to change Joseph, who was now quite happily staring out of the pram at his surroundings; the dirty nappy tucked away in the bottom of the pram until they came across a bin. A firework exploded in the sky overhead and Joseph clapped his hands and laughed at the shooting colours in the darkening sky.

She approached the Blue Bridge again. She saw two police officers on horseback.

As she drew near, one of them said, 'You haven't seen anything suspicious up there, have you?'

'No,' Emily said.

'You do know there's an escaped convict on the run?'

'Yes, I heard,' Emily said.

'It's best that you weren't out,' the police officer said. 'Especially by yourself… He could be anywhere.'

'I was looking for my cat.'

More fireworks went off from the opposite bank of the river.

'It's not a good night for a cat to be out,' the police officer said. 'It should be locked inside…'

'I could say the same for your escaped convict,' Emily said under her breath.

Joseph was staring up at the horses with wonder. Then another firework went off, a string of colours appearing in the darkening sky.

'Ohhhh,' Joseph said and clapped his hands together.

'You get yourselves home,' the police officer said to Emily. 'Your cat's probably there waiting for you.'

'I was thinking the same,' Emily said.

'And you haven't seen anything suspicious up there?'

Emily glanced back the way she had come.

'There was smoke,' she said, 'coming out of an old building, up there on the left.'

'How far?'

Emily gestured into the distance. 'Back there,' she said. 'Not far. Five minute walk at most.'

'We'd better check it out,' the police officer said, and the two mounted officers trotted past Emily and Joseph towards the Well House.

Theodore heard the clack of hooves approaching. He smelled the musk of the horses' coats. He looked across at Milton, who was putting on his now dry clothes and shoes.

The fire had died down but wisps of smoke still curled from it and out through the entrance of the Well House.

He miaowed at Milton that the police were on their way and no doubt they would be interested in what was the cause of the smoke from this old well.

'You shut it,' Milton said. 'I've told you…'

But Theodore carried on miaowing, staring at the entrance to the Well House.

'Horses?' Milton said, hearing the clacking of hooves. 'Well, why didn't you say? I think it's time we made a move…'

Milton pulled on his shoes and got to his feet.

The horses were almost at the Well House.

Theodore realised that if they didn't make it out, Milton would be arrested with no chance to get away.

But then what about his brother Miles? Only Milton knew of his brother's evil plot. With Milton put back inside, there would be nobody to stop him. Theodore didn't know what Miles looked like. He had to make sure that Milton stayed free long enough to stop his brother.

Theodore could smell the musk of the horses grew stronger. They were almost upon them. He slipped through the metal bars of the Well House gate. But it was too late.

The mounted police were already in front of them. There were two enormous beasts, their hooves capable of smashing the life out of him with one blow. Behind him he heard a rusty squeak as Milton swung open the metal gate, ready to make his escape.

Theodore raised his tail high. His fur stood on end, making him appear bigger than he was. He stared into the big dark brown eyes of the horse that loomed over him. He opened his mouth and hissed.

The horse looked down and noticed the small furry animal at her feet. Something inside her told her it would be a mistake to harm this creature that some humans took into their homes. The rider on her back urged her on, but he didn't know about the cat in front of her. So she reared up on her hind legs and whinnied.

The police officer was caught unaware and lost his balance, grabbing onto his colleague. They both fell to the ground.

Theodore looked on as the riderless horses whinnied excitedly and the riders began to get to their feet. I didn't know I had it in me, he thought.

'Quick,' Milton said. 'This is our chance.'

He slipped out of the Well House and darted back along the path. Theodore set off after him.

The police officer got up from the ground. 'Not sure what got into her,' Paul said, helping his colleague to her feet.

'Something must have spooked her,' Maria said grabbing the reins of her horse.

Wisps of smoke were still coming from the Well House.

'We'd better check out that building,' Maria said. 'It must have been what the woman with the pram was on about.'

She drew her horse over and peered inside.

'Anything in there?'

'There's a fire. An empty bag of sweets… Looks like they might be marshmallows. Some burnt sticks…'

'Sounds like kids,' Paul said. 'They must have scarpered when they heard us coming.'

'Here, hold this,' Maria said, handing her horse's reins to her colleague. 'There's something else…'

She stooped down and pulled open the metal grill.

'What is it?' Paul said.

'Only one of those Guy Fawkes masks. One of those that the protesters are all wearing.'

'There's going to be trouble tonight; I can feel it in my bones.'

'They've bussed up a thousand of them from London to cause trouble. Anarchists. Radicalists. Animal rights activists, badger baiters, Radiohead fans… You name it. We've got it coming.'

'We've got twenty extra officers from Leeds, mainly PCSOs. It's a bloody joke. If it kicks off, how are we going to cope?'

'And on top of everything, we have an escaped convict on the loose…'

'I did hear that if things get out of hand, they are going to issue us with Heckler and Koch water blasters.'

'I've always wanted to have a go with one of them. Wash the stupid grins off their faces!'

'Well, let's hope it doesn't come to that.'

Maria shook her head. 'I say we get them all in a narrow street like the Shambles and teapot them.'

'You mean 'kettle' them, don't you?'

'Isn't that what I said? Kettling… Tea-potting… Tea-bagging… Aren't they the same thing?'

'I think tea-bagging might have another meaning,' Paul said. 'Are you sure you didn't bang your head when you fell?'

Maria raised a hand to her helmet. 'I don't think so.'

'All this talk of teapots and kettles, how about we have a nice cup of tea,' Paul said. 'I brought my flask. A cup of Yorkshire Tea and you'll feel right as rain again.'

'A proper brew,' Maria said. 'Now you're talking!'

'I double-bagged it,' Paul said, undoing his knapsack to get to his flask.

'Well, better to be safe than sorry.'

'I meant my flask,' Paul said. 'I put two teabags in it.'

'Sorry,' Maria said, 'I thought you were talking about something else.'

The Pub That Famously Floods

The Kings Arms on King's Staith is a public house famous for flooding. Whenever York floods, which is quite regularly, library images of the pub are shown on the television news. But the pub located next to Ouse Bridge is well prepared for such flood events.

It has been well and truly flood-proofed. Electric points are at least four feet off the ground. Soft furnishings and furniture can be quickly removed to higher ground, to be returned once flood levels go down.

However, as the pub is so famous for being flooded, tourists expect it to be flooded all year round. They arrive with their wellies on, and the pub does not disappoint. The pub now retains the floodwater year round, so customers have to wade to the bar.

Theodore peered through the window from the stone windowsill. Milton was standing beside him, also looking in.

There were several regulars sitting on bar stools, their boots dangling in the black water that stood two feet above the floor. Tourists and out-of-towners had also come prepared, wearing waders and waterproofs, taking photographs of themselves with their feet below water. Sodden beermats floated on the water's surface. In the corner by the door, there was a flood marker, showing the highest levels the floodwaters had reached.

2000 had been a particularly good year, Theodore noted. If you were into flooding, which he certainly wasn't.

A customer at the bar, his back to them, ordered a pint of lager and a bag of pork scratchings. The landlord tossed a bag of deep-fried pieces of pig fat onto the bar and then went to pour the pint. But the barrel was almost empty and the glass was left with just an inch of foam in it.

'Can you go down and change the barrel?' the landlord said to the barman.

The barman looked up from his book. 'I'm reading,' he said.

'That's not a book,' the landlord said. 'That's a comic.' He laughed.

'It's not a comic,' the barman said. 'It's a graphic novel.'

'It's got pictures in it. Therefore it's a comic. Now go and change the barrel.'

The barman snapped his book closed.

Theodore noted the Guy Fawkes mask on the cover and the title 'V for Vendetta'. He wasn't a fan of graphic novels either; he preferred paw-etry.

The barman put on a diver's mask and strapped tanks onto his back. He opened a trapdoor in the floor. Then he dropped down into the flooded cellar to change the barrel.

The customer at the bar, who had ordered the pint of bitter, held up something brown between his thumb and forefinger. 'I have a pig's nipple in my pork scratchings,' he said.

'Not so loud,' the landlord said with a laugh, 'everyone will want one.'

'It's not a laughing matter,' the man said. 'I paid 79p for them.'

'There's probably a phone number on the back of the packet,' the landlord said. 'If you want to complain, complain to them…'

'I might do just that,' the man said.

He had a rucksack perched on the barstool next to him. He unzipped a side pocket and removed a mobile phone. He scrutinised the back of the packet of pork scratchings and then tapped a phone number into his mobile.

He swivelled round on his stool and placed the mobile to his ear.

'It's Miles!' Milton said, still peering through the window. 'What a stroke of luck!'

Theodore stared at the man with the mobile phone.

'I have a pig's nipple in my pork scratchings,' the man complained.

He remembered the man with the rucksack from outside the Yummy Fried Chicken, the litter lout with mayonnaise on his chin. So this was Miles: Milton's older brother. The one who might be plotting some terrible event for this evening.

'It's not a laughing matter,' Miles said. 'I paid 79p for them.'

Milton was already making his way to the front door. Theodore jumped down and followed Milton.

On the door of the pub was a large sign that read, 'Don't Open this Door! Use Side Door!'

But Milton didn't read the sign. He opened the door and the floodwater poured out onto King's Staith to be reunited with the Ouse.

Theodore braced himself as a tidal wave of black water passed over him. When he opened his eyes, he spied Milton standing in the entrance to the pub, his trousers drenched from the waist down.

'Look what you've gone and done!' the landlord shouted. 'You've only gone and let the floodwater out...'

Milton ignored the landlord. 'You!' he shouted across the bar room at Miles.

Miles, recognising his brother, smiled to himself. Then he slipped his mobile phone into his jeans, grabbed his rucksack and made for the side entrance.

Milton was straight after him.

'Not so fast!' the landlord shouted, his hand on Milton's shoulder.

Milton spun round and hit the landlord across the head with his fist.

The landlord went down and hit the wet floor.

The barman stuck his head up out of the trapdoor, removed his breathing apparatus and said, 'the water's going down.'

Theodore looked him in the face, eye to eye. You don't say.

'Did you not lock the front door?' the landlord shouted, still lying on the floor. 'I've told you a thousand times. The front door must always be kept locked… Otherwise something like this will happen!'

Then Miles slipped out of the side door, Milton close behind him.

As the barman struggled up through the trapdoor, Theodore noticed something small and brown on the stone floor in front of him. It was the sodden deep-fried pig's nipple. Theodore wondered for a moment whether to eat it or not. He decided not.

Outside he heard footfalls on cobblestones passing by the front entrance of the pub.

He glanced again at the pig's nipple and then made for the door.

As he exited onto King's Staith, he turned to see Miles taking the stone steps up to Low Ousegate, two at a time.

Milton was not far behind. But on reaching the bottom of the steps he stopped.

Theodore looked back up at Miles. Miles slowed down as he passed between two police officers standing at the top of the steps. Then he disappeared into the crowd, many of whom were wearing Guy Fawkes masks.

Milton turned away. He met Theodore's questioning gaze. Then he held his hands up to his face. He had left his Guy Fawkes mask behind, Theodore realised; back in the Well House. The police would no doubt recognise the escaped convict. Milton could not continue the pursuit. The police would recognise him and arrest him again. He would be back at Full Sutton by nightfall.

Milton turned and retreated towards Theodore, a look of hopelessness in his eyes.

Theodore walked forwards to meet Milton. When they were a couple of feet apart, Theodore sidestepped him and continued towards the steps.

He knew what Miles looked like. If Milton could not follow him and stop his brother's Bonfire Night Plot, it was down to him.

Don't do it, came the voice of the cat basket. *You have no idea what you're getting yourself caught up in. Miles is probably just going to let some fireworks off… You should keep out of it and come home. Bonfire Night is not a night for pets to be out. It's a night to stay at home and be glad you're not outside…*

Do be quiet, thought Theodore. I have to stop this man.

His tail held aloft, though sodden and bedraggled, he made his way across the wet cobbles towards the stone steps.

Battle of the Buskers

As you may know, the collective term for buskers is a cacophony. In recent years a cacophony of buskers has descended on Coney Street, many of them with very little talent. Some of them have also brought amplifiers in order to compete sonically with their neighbours and amplify their lack of talent.

As Miles passed the Spurriergate centre, he noticed the old guy on the stool with his guitar. He hadn't seen him for maybe twenty years. Back then he had two Border Collies; they would whine and howl at appropriate parts of the song. He used to have a blow-up doll dressed up in ladies clothes beside him. His little entourage had a name too. On a rectangle of cardboard, he had printed Heartbreak Candy.

'More like Deadbeat Cranky,' his father had muttered as they passed by one day.

The teenage Miles had paused to watch the performance. The busker had been playing *How Much Is That Doggy in the Window*, and after every time he sang the title, the two dogs would begin whining and barking. Miles thought it very clever. He had a fifty pence piece, his weekly pocket money, in his trouser pocket. He reached in and withdrew the coin.

The busker finished the song and people approached and threw coins into the guitar case on the ground. Miles looked at the coin in his hand and then at the guitar case. Then he felt his father's hand on his shoulder.

'Don't you be giving your money away,' his father Maxwell said.

Miles looked up at Maxwell.

'You go giving it away,' Maxwell said, 'and you'll never have any. It doesn't grow on trees.'

Miles nodded and slipped the coin back into his pocket.

Over forty years later, the middle-aged Miles noticed that the busker no longer had the dogs or the doll. He no longer had the Heartbreak Candy sign. His band was no more. There was just an old man struggling to be heard above the noise of the rival buskers.

He was playing *The Man Who Sold the World*, the Bowie song that Nirvana had nailed, many, many years ago. Both Bowie and Kurt Cobain were dead, Miles thought, but this busker, who had been, or he had supposed had been, old when he was just a boy, was still alive. In fact the old busker didn't look any older now than he did forty years ago. How did that work? Miles wondered.

Miles stopped in front of the busker, thinking about aging and death. He didn't notice the grey cat that had darted into the doorway behind the busker.

Theodore stared across at Miles. He noticed that Miles was mouthing along to the song, deep in thought. When the song ended, he reached into his pocket and plucked out a silver coin. He approached the busker and dropped the 50 pence coin into the guitar case. He turned and walked away.

Theodore followed.

Further down Coney Street, there was a Tina Turner tribute act. She was singing along to Private Dancer. Miles didn't stop and give her any money. She wasn't even singing in tune.

Then there was a group of students, playing to a large crowd. They even had a drum kit set up in the street.

They were playing *Don't Look Back in Anger*, as Miles walked past.

'Don't look on with languor…' Theodore thought he heard him say.

Miles paused in front of the Starbucks on the corner of Coney Street and New Street.

This building used to be a branch of the National Westminster Bank. It was where his father Maxwell had begun his career, aged 16, as a clerk; before he had departed for London and a career in investment banking; a career that Miles would also pursue.

On the building's corner, there was still the sculpted, red and gold coat of arms, with boars standing on either side of a shield that bore three boars' heads and the motto *PRODESSE CIVIBUS*. Maxwell had told Miles that the boars symbolised hospitality and the motto meant 'to benefit the citizens'.

His father had evidently been misguided. Boars were far from hospitable, from what Miles knew about them, and banks were not set up to benefit the citizens; they were created to benefit the bankers.

He glanced at St Martin's clock, which overhangs Coney Street; the Little Admiral standing on top, pointing his strange instrument at the sky. It was almost five o'clock. It was time he had tea.

As he turned right into St Helen's Square, he was almost run over by a pram.

'Hey!' he shouted at the young mum. 'Watch where you're going!'

He stepped around the pram and carried on his way with an angry shake of his head.

Emily stood and let the crowd pass around her. What was it they said about never feeling more alone than when in a crowd?

Then baby Joseph began to gripe. She was going to have to find somewhere to feed him.

She took her mobile phone from her coat pocket. She had a new message. She opened it.

'Theo not here,' Jonathan had texted. 'Have you had any luck?'

She messaged back. 'No. Nothing. I am really worried now.'

Before she could put her mobile away, Jonathan messaged back. 'Come home.'

'But what about Theo?'

'He'll come back when he's ready.'

'He's probably terrified. I can't believe he's disappeared on Bonfire Night.'

'He'll be hiding somewhere… I think you should come home now. It's getting dark.'

'I can't,' Emily texted back. 'Not until I find Theo.'

Then she put her mobile back in her pocket.

Joseph looked at her and sucked his thumb and Emily knew that she would have to find somewhere to feed him.

Theodore had lost Miles in the crowded street. He took refuge in the doorway of an empty shop. He stared out at the passing people, trying to locate the man with the rucksack.

Then he heard a whisper above the noise of the crowd. 'That way,' it murmured. 'He went that way.'

Theodore looked across the street. On the second floor windowsill of the building facing him there was a sculpture of a black cat.

The cat had been installed on the windowsill by York architect Tom Adams in 1979. In the same way that Leonardo da Vinci signed his sketches with a mouse, Tom Adams bestowed a cat upon the buildings he worked on. These days there are many Tom Adams cats adorning the city's buildings and more erected after his death in 2006 by others wanting to carry on the tradition.

'He went that way,' the cat sculpture murmured to Theodore, flicking its tail further down Coney Street.

Theodore blinked his eyes in disbelief; there is a lot I do not understand about this world, he thought.

He emerged from the dark doorway and carried on down the street in the direction that the stone cat had flicked its tail.

Up ahead he spotted Emily pushing Joseph in his pram. Her face was creased with worry. Her eyes darted from left to right but she failed to see him. He stopped in his tracks. He watched as she passed by. He turned round and watched as she disappeared among the crowd. He had to carry on the pursuit. He turned and made his way into St Helen's Square.

Another busking band was playing and a large crowd had formed, many of whom were wearing Guy Fawkes masks, others were wearing cow or badger masks.

He tried to navigate a way through the hundreds of feet. A cigarette end landed in front of him and he darted to the side, narrowly avoiding the smouldering butt. A toddler in red wellies spotted him and made towards him stamping his little feet. Fortunately the child was reined in before he could stomp on Theodore.

Theodore closed his eyes a moment. He wished for an empty bedroom. A windowsill in the sunshine. A laundry basket of newly-dried and folded clothes, preferably woollens. He wished for his cat basket by the radiator in the kitchen of his home. He wished he was far from this madding crowd.

I told you so, the voice of the cat basket said. *You should never have left the safety of home. What did you hope to achieve?*

The humans will always wreak havoc upon the outside world. They cannot be stopped.

The humans will eventually destroy themselves by their selfish and destructive nature. But until that day comes, you must wait. You must wait patiently until you hear the call.

Theodore opened his eyes, only to see a large burgundy Dr Marten's boot about to come down on his head. He dashed to the right but the boot landed on his tail. He cried out in pain: Bastet!

He took refuge in the doorway of the Edinburgh Woollen Mill, beneath a rack of woolly jumpers. He took the opportunity to examine his tail. It was kinked. His wonderful tail was deformed; he would never be able to hold it up with pride again. He already had a torn ear that folded down on itself: the result of a feline skirmish in a previous adventure. If this went on, his handsome looks would be gone with his youth.

He peered back at the crowded square. He needed to get back out there or he would lose track of Miles. He crossed the shop entrance and hugged the side of Bettys Café Tea Rooms. There was a queue that snaked around the corner. Even the rain did not deter people from a tea at the renowned Bettys. He watched as Miles walked past the queue. He darted after him. Between the shoes and boots he ran. He was closing in on him.

Then he stopped. Miles had entered Bettys.

Sand Dogs

Milton walked down High Ousegate and stopped in front of a stall that had been set up in front of the Spurriergate Centre. The stall sold cheap plastic Guy Fawkes masks, aimed at those attending the march that evening. The plastic mask had become an icon of popular culture, used to protest around the world against tyranny and the status quo. Cashing in on anti-capitalism, Milton thought with a sneer.

He asked how much the masks were.

Five pounds, he was told by the Chinese man. They probably cost five pence to produce in Asia, Milton thought, remembering he didn't have any money.

A teenager approached and also asked how much the masks were. As he was rummaging in his coat pockets, Milton snatched one of the masks and began to make his way into the crowded street. But he'd been spotted.

'Tony!' a Chinese woman shrieked. 'He's taken one without paying…'

Milton heard footsteps behind him. He turned and raised his fist.

Tony came to a halt in front of the raised fist. He had only paid fifty pounds for a thousand masks. Five pence each. He had taken over five hundred pounds already and sales were increasing as the day went on and the streets became more crowded. He looked at the clenched fist held inches in front of his face.

Then he heard his wife Sue yell from behind him, 'Get it off him! He is a thief!'

Tony thought of the bills he had to pay. His daughters were at the Mount School. Not only had he the school fees to pay but also the costs for boarding. Then there would be their university fees to come. It was not easy having girls at the Mount School.

'Police! Police!' Sue screamed from behind him.

Tony felt a bead of sweat trickle down his face. Was it worth being hit in the face over five pounds? He took a step backwards, away from the man with the clenched fist and troubled stare.

'Take it,' Tony said. 'Please just take the mask.'

Milton lowered his fist. He turned and walked away, snapping the Guy Fawkes mask over his face.

Sue screamed, 'Don't let him get away! Police! Police!'

'Let it go,' Tony said. 'We have plenty more.'

'That's not the point,' Sue snapped. 'It's the principle. Whatever would the twins think if they knew what you were really like? Weak! That's what you are! Weak! Weak! Weak!'

'That's enough, Sue,' Tony said, walking back to his makeshift stall, where a queue of people had begun to form. 'Enough…'

The streets were crowded but Milton knew that Miles was carrying a large rucksack. He couldn't be hard to spot in the crowd.

He noticed that British Home Stores had closed down. An Eastern European man was squatting down in front of the empty shop. He had created a dog out of sand. Milton was impressed.

This young man had taken a bag of sand and with only a little knife he had created a sculpture of a labrador. What skill and talent had gone into that? The young man was making the final touches to the dog's head, absorbed in his task, a little pile of sand in front of him.

Milton reached into his pocket but remembered he had no money.

The young man looked up at him. He tilted his head at the little basket next to him that was half full of coins. His eyes were full of hope.

Milton raised his palms. He would have liked to help this young man who had such great talent. Such potential! No doubt he would go on to succeed in life. A life in which he had so terribly failed.

The young man, understanding that Milton wasn't going to give him any money, turned away and carried on with his monumental work.

Milton turned away, an ache in his heart.

He turned right into New Street, then up Davygate towards Parliament Street.

By the side of the disabled toilet in St Sampson's Square, he noticed another sculpture of a dog created out of sand. That's some coincidence, he thought, approaching the young man.

The sculpture was again of a Labrador, identical to the one he had seen on Coney Street.

Then it dawned on him. The sculptures were not the hand of the young men. They probably were plastic shells with a coating of sand stuck on. It was a con and he had been fooled.

He looked at the little basket of coins by the man's side. 'You're a fraud,' he said.

The young man, who had been pretending to make some final touches to the dog's face, turned. 'Excuse me?'

'This,' Milton said, tapping the dog with the toe of his shoe, 'is a fraud.'

'I not understand you.'

'You did not make this,' Milton said. He tapped the sand dog again with his foot, so that it moved two inches. 'You are a fraud!'

'Please, no!'

'It's a con!' Milton said.

He looked at the people around him. They were staring at him.

'Don't you understand? He hasn't made this. He's conning you. He's a fraud!'

A middle-aged man tutted, dropped a pound coin in the basket of coins and walked away.

Probably a Liberal, Milton thought. He shook his head. 'Don't you understand? It's all a con. The sand dogs aren't real!'

He raised his foot and brought it down on the sand dog. The plastic shell crumpled beneath his foot. 'See! I told you...'

'You are an ass hole man,' the young man said, a tremor in his voice. He got to his feet and faced Milton.

Milton pushed his Guy Fawkes mask to the top of his head. 'And you are a liar and a cheat.'

Milton assessed his opponent. Although skinny, he was taller, younger and fitter than he was. Maybe he shouldn't have picked a fight with this guy.

Then he heard a voice to his right. 'It's him,' a woman's voice said. 'The escaped convict...'

'You sure?' a man's voice said.

'Yes, I'm sure. I remember his face off the telly. And he's wearing the clothes they said on the radio. A red and black checked shirt. I remember.'

Milton turned to face them.

'It is him! Milton Macavity!' the woman shrieked. 'Police!'

Milton felt a hundred eyes upon him.

He turned and began to run through the crowd. But he soon tired. He bent over, trying to get his breath back. Life on the inside had left him badly out of shape. His jeans felt cold and wet on his legs, the result of his second soaking at the Kings Arms. He needed to get warm.

Back at home, Jonathan stood at the back door, a box of cat biscuits in his hand. He shook the box, so that the biscuits rattled inside.

'Theo! Theo!' he called.

But Theodore didn't come.

He walked across the kitchen and peered inside the cat basket for the twentieth time. 'The Cat Cave,' he liked to call it. One of Emily's old woollen jumpers was laid in the bottom, coated with Theodore's grey fur. He wondered if Theodore would ever find his way back to it.

He went again to the backdoor and opened it. He stepped outside and surveyed the yard.

He noticed the clothes line. Emily should have hung the clothes on the clothes horse in front of the radiator. They were as wet as when she had hung them out, several hours ago.

Then he noted that there were gaps on the clothes line… Gaps where his shirt and jeans had been.

Jonathan remembered Theodore miaowing at the transparent cat flap while he watched the news. That was when there was the newsflash that Milton Macavity had escaped from custody while at York Hospital.

He then noticed the green smock that lay discarded in a heap.

'Theo,' he said, shaking his head. 'What have you got yourself mixed up in this time?'

He knew he would have to return to town to find him.

He texted Emily, 'I'm coming back into town. I think Theo is in real trouble.'

His denim jacket was soaked through. He took it off and hung it over the kitchen radiator to dry. On his way out, he grabbed his brown corduroy jacket from the coat rack and then headed back into town.

Oliver Bartholomew Relapses

Emily had managed to find a table in the Spurriergate Centre, where she could feed Joseph. In his highchair, he played with his plastic spoon, flicking pureed parsnip at passers-by while Emily tapped away on her phone.

She requested to join a Facebook group called 'Pets – Lost & Found – York-UK'. Seconds later she was accepted. She selected a recent photograph of Theodore and then wrote, 'This is Theodore.' Her eyes blurred and she had to stop herself from crying. 'He's been missing since this morning,' she wrote. 'Haxby Road area. I'm so worried as it's Bonfire Night and he's out here somewhere…'

Joseph gurgled. She looked over and watched as a bubble of pureed parsnip appeared at the side of his mouth, only to pop a second later.

'If anyone sees him, let me know,' she typed and then posted it.

Seconds later her post had been shared several times by good-natured strangers.

Then a message arrived from Jonathan. She responded, saying, 'I'm at the Spurriergate Centre.'

'Stay there,' Jonathan texted back. 'I'll be with u in 20 mins.'

Emily returned to Facebook. She found another group. This one was called 'York C.R.U.D. – Cat Rescuers UniteD'. She requested to join this group too though it didn't sound as good.

Then she got a comment back from her first post.

'I saw a cat like this by Monk Bar. A homeless guy had him tied to a bit of string. He said it was called Smoky.'

Then someone else commented. 'I saw them too. He was begging for cat food. That's what the sign said.'

'I saw them in the Tesco on Goodramgate. The homeless guy was buying cider.'

'I know that guy. He drinks in the little churchyard off Goodramgate... Behind the Happy Valley Chinese restaurant. He's a proper pisshead.'

The homeless guy on the bench, Emily thought. He must have taken Theodore and used him for begging. She swore under her breath; then she called her dad.

Patrick put his mobile on the kitchen side and took a bottle of Chablis from the wine rack. He poured himself a large glass. He then went into the den, where Oliver was sitting on the sofa, wearing Patrick's second-best dressing gown, a mug of tea on the coffee table in front of him.

Oliver's face lit up when he saw Patrick holding the glass of wine. 'Can I have a glass?' he asked.

'No,' Patrick said and took a large gulp of wine.

'But that's not fair,' Oliver said.

'Life's not fair, Oliver,' Patrick said gravely. And then, 'Did you take my daughter's cat?'

'Cat?' Oliver scratched at his head. His overgrown hair was still wet from the bath Patrick had run for him. 'I didn't steal any cat.'

'People saw you with him, Oliver. You were out begging with my daughter's cat.'

'*That* cat? It was your daughter's? I had no idea... I just borrowed him for a couple of hours.'

'Yes, it was my daughter's cat... And she is now frantic with worry. Now tell me: when and where did you last see the cat.'

'In the churchyard where you found me. It got away from me and ran off.'

'And that was the last time you saw him?'

'Yes, that's right. Now how about that glass of wine? I've told you all I know.'

'You are not allowed any wine,' Patrick said sternly. 'I have made you a mug of Taylor's finest Yorkshire Tea. From now on, you will drink only tea. You are teetotal while you are in this house. If you relapse, you will be out. Back on the streets. Do you understand me?'

'Yes,' Oliver said. 'I understand.'

Patrick put his half-empty glass of wine down on the coffee table. 'I have given you a great opportunity… don't forget. This could be the beginning of the rest of your life. If you want it to be…'

Oliver nodded, staring at the cream pile of the carpet.

'Now, I am going to call my daughter and let her know what you have told me.'

Patrick turned and left the den.

Back in the kitchen, he called Emily's mobile. 'It *was* Theodore,' he said. 'Oliver borrowed him for a couple of hours, for financial gain. Theo managed to escape from him.'

'Does he know where he is now?' Emily asked.

'Last time Oliver saw him was back in the churchyard.'

'Jonathan's on his way back into town,' Emily said. 'We are going to keep searching for him… He's still in the city centre, I know it. I'm not going home till I find him.'

'Tell her she needs to get herself and Joseph back home,' Trish said. 'Theo will find his own way home. There's trouble brewing in York tonight.'

'Your mum says…' Patrick began.

'I heard,' Emily said.

She heard the chinking of pots in the sink; then her mother in the background saying, 'All this fuss over a cat.'

She could picture the scene. Her mother standing in front of the kitchen sink, her apron spotless as she did the washing up. Her father standing by the Welsh dresser, mobile phone in hand. Bess, the border collie, lying in her basket. It was the perfect world she had grown up in. She raised her hand to her head. She felt something wet. It was parsnip, beginning to harden in her hair. She looked at Joseph. He was splatting his food with his hands on the plastic tray in front of him and grinning like a little demon. Her world was so less than perfect.

Her dad was saying, 'He'll turn up. I know he will,' in an attempt to reassure her.

'I know,' she said. 'I have to go now.'

She hung up and started to cry.

Back in the Patrick's den, Oliver stared at the glass of wine that Patrick had left on the coffee table. He picked it up and took a tiny sip. Then another sip. Then a gulp. Then it was empty.

Scenes from a Swiss-Yorkshire Restaurant

Frederick (Dickie) Belmont, a Swiss confectioner in search of his fortune, arrived at King's Cross railway station in London and accidently got onto a Yorkshire-bound train. He never looked back.

It wasn't long before Dickie opened his first Bettys Café in Harrogate in 1919. Why it was called Bettys, nobody knows for sure. One story has it that during a meeting by the directors to discuss the choice of names, a child accidently wandered in. When asked her name, she said Betty. ''That'll do,' Dickie said. 'Bettys it is!'

By 1927 afternoon tea was being served and ten years later Dickie opened the famous Bettys Café Tea Rooms on St Helen's Square in York. The interiors of Bettys were inspired by the rooms of the Queen Mary ocean liner; Dickie and his wife Claire had been on its maiden voyage the previous year. If you like wood panelling, it's *the* place to go.

These days tourists queue round the corner in all weathers to have the Bettys experience. Miles strode past the queue and into the shop. He didn't believe in queuing.

He glanced at the counters. They were selling off Halloween stock: gingerbread bats, ghost-shaped lebkuchen and chocolate pumpkins. He spotted a basket of Fat Rascals. He used to like them when he was a kid.

He took his rucksack off and held it by the handle at the top. He looked back at the queue that snaked out

of the door. He strode over and pushed his way in near to the front.

'Excuse me!' an old man said. 'There is a queue.'

Miles glared at him. 'I know. I'm in it, aren't I?'

A woman tugged at the man's coat sleeve. 'Don't make a fuss,' she hissed.

The man held his tongue, not wanting to make a scene.

Theodore navigated the many pairs of feet. He made it into the shop part of Bettys without being seen. He saw Miles being led to a table inside the tea rooms. He followed.

He kept close to the wall. He too bypassed the queue. He was with Miles on that one: the day you see cats waiting in an orderly fashion for their food is surely a day that will never come.

He could see dozens of tables, all covered with bright white table cloths that reached almost to the floor. If he could make it inside, he could hide below the tables and make his way from table to table until he located Miles by his footwear; he remembered Miles was wearing shiny black brogues. Then he could find out what was in the rucksack.

He chose his moment. Any moment was as good as any other, wasn't it? He dashed into the tea rooms. He made it below the nearest table and was met by a pair of shiny red shoes. There was no commotion. He had done it. Now he just had to locate Miles and his rucksack.

He peered out at the nearby tables. He would have to make his way to the next table.

Again he chose his moment and dashed below another table. This one had several pairs of shoes but no shiny black brogues.

A waitress went over to the duty manager. 'I think there's a cat under table 47,' she said.

'A cat? In the tea rooms?'

'Yes, I saw it. It dashed from table 14 to table 47. I don't think any of the customers saw it.'

'But how did it get in?'

'I don't know.'

'We need to get it out,' the duty manager said. 'Before someone notices it. Leave it to me.'

The duty manager approached table 47. 'Is everything satisfactory?' she said, stooping and tilting her head to try and see under the table.

Theodore positioned himself in the centre of the table.

'Could we see the desserts' trolley,' a voice said.

'Yes, of course,' another voice said. 'I'll have it sent over straight away.'

Miles was sitting by the rain-specked window. He hadn't been in Bettys for over twenty years. Then he had been with his brother Milton and his father Maxwell. It was the lunch that had decided their fates.

Memories slowly surfaced.

He had ordered the chicken schnitzel. He always ordered the chicken schnitzel when he had dinner with his father Maxwell and his younger brother Milton on the first Sunday of each month. That was how often he saw his father. Once a month. Twelve times a year.

That day, they all had ordered the chicken schnitzel. When the waiter had brought out the three plates, one cradled into his elbow, he had dropped Milton's. The chicken schnitzel ended up on the floor, cheesy side down. Milton looked down at it, a lump in his throat. The waiter promised to return shortly with a new one.

'Well, there's no point in letting ours go cold,' Maxwell said and proceeded to tuck in.

Miles did likewise and they had both almost finished their meals before a replacement chicken schnitzel could be brought for Milton.

Miles realised that Milton, ever the sensitive one, looked like he was about to cry. He smiled to himself and then popped a very thin chip into his mouth.

'There is something I've been meaning to tell you,' Maxwell began, his voice serious. 'Something I've been meaning to tell you for quite some time, as a matter of fact.'

Miles knew that their father had an important job in the City but wasn't exactly sure what he did. He knew he commuted from the London suburbs but wasn't exactly sure what suburb. He knew that his father lived with someone down in London but wasn't exactly sure with whom. There was a lot he didn't know about his father; he had never taken the time to ask.

'Well, I think the time has come that you know some home truths,' Maxwell said. 'I feel that this has dragged on for far too long.'

'Well, what is it?' Miles asked.

'I am going to divorce your dipsomaniac mother and then marry my partner Cheryl. I am fed up of living a lie. Up to this point in my life that is what my life has been… A lie. And that has got to change.'

Just then the waiter reappeared with Milton's replacement chicken schnitzel. He slid it in front of him and said, 'I'm sorry.'

Miles wondered if he was apologising for the dropped schnitzel or for the state of their parents' relationship. The waiter turned and walked back to the kitchen doors.

'You will be starting at university in London,' Maxwell said, looking at his elder son. 'So perhaps we could meet up for lunch from time to time. You could meet Cheryl.'

'I don't know who Cheryl is,' Miles said. 'First I've heard of her.'

Maxwell turned to his younger son. 'I'm afraid you will have to go to York College and take your A levels there. I am not prepared to pay the fees for St Peter's for another two years. Like I said: I feel that this has dragged on for far too long already. Running two households takes its toll. And I am not prepared to do it any longer.'

Milton stared at his plate of food, the chicken schnitzel untouched.

'Don't look so glum,' Maxwell said. 'When I was your age, I was already working. I didn't have the benefit of a private education. You need to make your own way in this world.'

Milton didn't say anything.

Miles broke the silence. 'I didn't know you had a woman down there,' he said.

Maxwell looked at his elder son. He nodded. 'Yes, I do. We have cohabited for over ten years. Your mother knows.'

Miles noticed that his father's face was the colour of gammon. He hoped he wouldn't develop such a reddened face with age. But he did take after his father. He had the same dark brown hair and eyes. He glanced over at his ginger-haired brother, the chicken schnitzel left untouched in front of him.

'Shall we have dessert?' Maxwell said.

Milton got up from the table. 'I have to go out,' he said.

Miles looked out of the plate glass window and saw his younger brother hurry off in the direction of the Museum Gardens.

'I think Milton hasn't taken it very well,' Maxwell said. 'We'd better go after him.'

That day had been the turning point in Miles's life. It had been a day of fateful consequences.

Twenty-odd years later Miles gazed out of the window and wondered how lives can be decided so trivially.

'Are you ready to order?' a waitress asked.

Miles turned. 'Sorry,' he said. 'I was a million miles away.'

'I can give you some more minutes if you like?'

He looked at the waitress in her starched white apron and white long-sleeved blouse. She looked like something from an Agatha Christie television adaptation.

He glanced down at the menu. He hadn't even opened it; his mind had been absorbed in the past.

'The chicken schnitzel,' Miles said, 'and a pot of Tea Room Blend.'

The waitress scribbled in her pad and then left.

Miles got to his feet. He picked up his rucksack and carried it with him downstairs. He needed to make some final adjustments.

Theodore noticed the shiny black brogues as they passed by the table he was hiding under. He crossed to the edge of the table but there were several waiters walking up and down, trying to peer under tables; they were on to him, he realised. He didn't know where Miles was going but he was going to have to follow. He couldn't let him get away.

Then he saw his chance. The sweets' trolley was being pushed between the tables, laden with Fat Rascals, chocolate tortes, frangipane, eclairs, tarts and brightly coloured macaroons. The trolley had a shelf a few inches above the floor. Transportation, Theodore thought. As the trolley passed by his table, he hopped on board.

He heard a voice nearby say, 'Russell. I think this wine has gone to my head…'

'But you've only had the one glass, Barbara…'

'But I've just seen a large grey cat riding the cake trolley!'

'It must be your medication,' Russell said, 'mixing with the alcohol… We'd better get you back to Scarborough.'

Death of a Dickman

Randy Dickman had been handicapped by his unfortunate name his whole life.

There are others with even worse names. There is a resident of Los Angeles called Russell Wankum, a Belgian politician called Luc Anus and a Arun Dikshit living in San Jose. If you are a Wilson or Smith, you should feel grateful.

But Randy was loath to change his name as he was named after his paternal grandfather, who had been a hero during World War Two. Like many American and Canadian fighter pilots, he had been stationed outside of York and flown many missions over Germany. He had eventually got shot down one night over Cologne, his body never recovered.

His grandson Randy was looking for Dickmen in the mirror at Bettys.

During the war the mirror had been upstairs in Bettys Bar. This was where the American and Canadian pilots stationed in Yorkshire drank between missions. They nicknamed the bar 'The Briefing Room' or 'The Dive'. Many pilots signed their names on the large mirror using the diamond-tipped pen set aside for that purpose. By the end of the war, the mirror contained 568 names, many belonging to dead pilots.

Randy had searched every inch of the mirror but had not been able to locate a Dickman among the silvery signatures. He had read that the mirror had been damaged during an air raid. The surviving sections had been taken down and put back up downstairs in what is now the corridor outside the toilets. Randy wondered if his grandfather had written his name on one of the sections that had been destroyed, his signature blown into a thousand thin splinters of glass.

He was examining a section of the mirror for the third time when he was jostled. He turned and saw a bulky blue rucksack heading towards the door of the gents'.

'Hey!' he called after the disappearing figure.

The person with the rucksack didn't even turn to acknowledge him. The toilet door closed silently behind the man.

Randy then made a split second decision that would cost him his life. He followed the man with the rucksack into the gents'.

Milton passed by the large window of Bettys. He halted at the corner and stared in through the rain-flecked glass. There in front of him was a table set for one. An untouched plate of chicken schnitzel, pommes allumettes, salad and roasted cherry tomatoes had been placed on the table along with a pot of tea for one. It was as though the place had been set for him. His stomach growled with hunger and his mind raced back to that Sunday when he had lunched with Miles and his father Maxwell for the last time; he had not entered Bettys since that eventful day.

He remembered looking down at his untouched plate of food while Miles and his father decided what they would have for dessert. He felt sick. He felt like he was actually going to throw up. Dessert… His father was deserting them.

He had always suspected that his father favoured Miles. Miles was like his father. He was more like his mother. His thoughts turned to his mother. She had probably been drinking since Maxwell had called round for them that morning. When they returned, she would be passed out on the chaise longue in the conservatory. 'Just having a nap,' she would slur. Then she would get up and fix herself another gin and tonic. It was so predictable.

That day, some twenty-odd years ago, he had left the tea rooms, his eyes blurred by tears, and made his way to the Museum Gardens. He needed to be by himself.

He walked through the gates and passed between two strutting peacocks, their feathers fanned out behind them. Fortunately the gardens were almost empty of people. He found a bench by the museum that looked down over the gardens towards the Ouse. Thoughts raced around his head. His father and brother were no doubt tucking into their desserts back in Bettys. Then his father would get the train back to London and carry on with his life down there. He realised that nobody cared about him. He closed his eyes and hugged himself. In the distance he saw the dark water of the River Ouse. He might as well throw himself in. His life was over before it had even started, he realised. He closed his eyes and wished he was already dead.

'What's the matter with you, young sir?' a man said. Milton opened his eyes. A tramp had joined him on the bench. He looked like what you would expect a tramp to look like. Red veined bulbous nose, large grey straggly beard, yellowed eyes. But his voice was more that of a gentleman.

'Do you want to talk about it?' the tramp said, leaning towards Milton. 'I can be a good listener.'

Milton shook his head.

'Well, I'm just going to sit here and enjoy the view. Don't mind me.'

The tramp reached into a carrier bag by his feet and took out a can of Special Brew. He cracked it open and took a large swig.

Milton looked at the man. He didn't seem to have a care in the world. He would probably just roll under a bush that evening and sleep beneath the stars. He glanced from the tramp's contented face, to the can of beer he held and then back to the tramp's face.

The tramp turned to face him. 'You want a can?'

Milton nodded.

His drinking up to that point had been largely confined to finishing off bottles of wine that his mother left out; she never seemed to realise. He had tried the gin and tonic she always had in the house but he hated the taste.

'You got any money,' the tramp said.

Milton reached into his jacket pocket and took out his wallet. He handed his new companion a crumpled five pound note. The tramp smiled and handed Milton a can of Special Brew.

After Milton had had a few sips, he began to tell his new friend his troubles. By the end of the first can, he felt his troubles receding into the distance; in fact, he struggled to remember why he had been so upset. By the end of the second can, he was having a good time. His troubles were gone and he was riding a wave of drunkenness, laughing at the absurdities of life. By the end of the third can, he was throwing up in the bushes, his new friend gone.

He staggered out of the Museum Gardens and into Museum Street, straight in front of the No.1 bus. What happened next was a blur.

He heard his father shout his name.

Then his father was lying beneath the driver's side front wheel, pinned to the road.

People were shouting. A child screamed. A crowd gathered. His brother Miles swore at him.

They tried to lift the bus off his father.

Milton looked on helplessly.

His father looked at him, the bus wheel on his chest. Then he said his surprising dying words: 'Sylvia…,' he said. Then: 'Please forgive me.' Then he died.

Sylvia was the name of Maxwell's estranged wife and Miles and Milton's mother.

'Look what you've gone and done,' Miles said, under his breath.

Milton turned to his brother.

Miles shook his head. He said, 'You've gone and killed dad.'

Tears streamed down Milton's cheeks.

The crowd backed away leaving the two brothers standing by their dead dad.

Then a peacock approached from the entrance of the Museum Gardens. It strutted into the empty circle in front of the bus. It looked at the dead man under the bus wheel. Then it screamed, 'Bu-kirk!'

A quarter of a century later, Milton stared through the eyeholes in his Guy Fawkes mask at the untouched plate of food on the table in Bettys. He had to find Miles and stop him. Whatever foul plot his brother had come up with, there was only Milton who could stand in his way.

So, with a knot of hunger and misery in his stomach, he turned and followed the crowd towards the Museum Gardens.

Theodore was downstairs, in a wood-panelled corridor lined with doors on one side and a mirror on the other. He located the gents'. He pushed against the door but it did not open. He heard footsteps behind him. He turned and saw two waiters, a man and a woman, coming towards him. He flattened himself into the door recess.

Then the door swung inwards. Theodore was inside the gents'. Before the door could close behind him, he saw Miles, rucksack on his back leaving. In the seconds before the door closed, Theodore heard the rucksack tick three times in three seconds. A ticking bag, he thought. There must be an alarm clock in it.

He looked at the closed door. He knew he had no means to open it from the inside. From the other side of the door, footsteps grew nearer.

Then there was a knock on the door and a voice called, 'Are we all right to come in? Hello? Hello?'

When nobody answered, the door swung open.

Theodore fled into one of the toilet cubicles. There was a partition separating his cubicle from the next. There was a gap below the partition about four inches high. From the next cubicle, a pool of blood had spread.

Then there were footsteps in front of the cubicle door. As the door was pushed open, Theodore ducked under the partition and into the next cubicle.

A silver-haired man lay slumped on the floor, his throat cut.

Theodore padded across the toilet floor, his paws dabbing at the pool of warm blood.

There was a rapping at this cubicle door.

'Please open the door!' a man called.

Theodore noticed that the door was locked from the inside. How the man had been murdered was a locked toilet cubicle mystery, but Theodore did not have time to try and figure it out.

Outside, someone was hammering on the door. 'I'm going to have to kick in this door,' the man said, 'if you don't open it now.'

Theodore didn't have long. He inspected his surroundings.

Behind the corpse, there was some boxing covering pipework. The boxing had a hatch in the corner for access. Theodore pushed at the hatch but it did not give. He realised that it must lift up and outwards. He then noticed a slot at the bottom, where someone could slot in a screwdriver and lift the hatch out.

Theodore went to work with his claws. He managed to prise out the hatch and lift it an inch but it fell back into place before he could get his head below it. The second time he managed to get his nose below it. There was more hammering on the door behind him. He pushed himself through and up into the boxing. He managed to pull his tail through behind him just as the cubicle door was kicked in from the outside.

There were some pipes running along the wall and a gap above them. He squeezed himself into this gap and crawled along. He turned a corner and the gap became wider and higher. He began to trot along the pipes.

But then the pipes plunged downwards and Theodore fell into darkness.

Subterranean York

Beneath York there is a network of underground tunnels built by the Romans some 1,600 years ago. This culverted drainage system is still operational in part today.

During the siege of York in the seventeenth century, legend tells that people were smuggled into and out of the city through this subterranean network of tunnels. Only a certain blind man knew his way about the unlit passageways. As he walked through the tunnels, he played a violin so that people could follow him in the dark.

Theodore opened his eyes. He could make out sandstone blocks on either side of him. Beneath him there was soft silt. At least he had had a soft landing. He peered upwards. There was a grey circle of light. There was no way he could scale the stone shaft and make his way back to the surface.

He was lying on a raised platform. Beside him there was a channel in which water trickled. He knew that all water flowed to the sea. If he followed the flow of the water, he would come out at the river. Theodore decided to go the other way. One dip in the Ouse was enough for him.

He got to his paws and began to make his way along the culvert. Side passages led off to the left and right, some of them were vaulted, others had flat slabs of Millstone Grit for a roof. In places, he had to wade through ancient silts, at other times he had to make way for rats that used the drainage system like an underground road network.

Smaller channels extended off this passage, many of them filled with dry soil. In one of them he spied a pile of bones. They were the remains of a slave child, sent down into the network of tunnels to clean them out, only to get lost and never find his way out again. Theodore plodded on, against the trickle of water.

Then he stopped. He looked up at the vaulted arch over his head. Emily was there, ten feet above his head. He couldn't see her, hear her or smell her; he just knew she was there; call it cat sense, if you like.

Theodore miaowed as loudly as he could.

A drop of cold water fell from the roof of the channel and landed on his head.

Emily stopped. She looked around her.

'He's here,' she said to Jonathan. 'I just know it.'

Jonathan had returned to the city centre to help look for Theodore. He looked around him but the streets were crowded and he knew that the chances of finding him, if he was in the middle of York, were small. A cat would undoubtedly find a quiet place, out of sight, and lay low until things died down. Any ordinary cat would not be in the middle of York on Bonfire Night of all nights. But Jonathan knew that Theodore was far from ordinary.

As they walked past Lendal Post Office, he said, 'Let's try the Museum Gardens. He might be hiding there.'

Emily agreed. 'Yes. Theodore's like me. Doesn't like crowds…'

There were many others heading towards the gardens. Many of them wore masks or horror make up. Among the many Guy Fawkes, there were zombies, witches, ghosts and ghouls, and others dressed up as cows and badgers. The odd local caught up in the melee wore a determined expression, wanting to be home before the Million Mask March started. The demonstration was scheduled to begin at six o'clock and converge on the Minster at nine o'clock.

As the crowd marched, they began to chant, 'One solution: revolution.'

'Let's hope there's no trouble,' Jonathan said.

'I doubt it,' Emily said. 'It's supposed to be a peaceful protest. They just want a fairer world. I think they are right about a lot of things. We need to think about what sort of world we are going to leave behind for our children, don't we?'

'You're right,' Jonathan said, 'but there's always a few who ruin it for the majority. A handful that will have come just to make trouble.'

'Let's hope nothing happens,' Emily said. 'I just want to find Theo and get home.'

'Isn't that your dad's car?' Jonathan said, as they approached the gates to the Museum Gardens. 'I thought they'd gone back to Acaster Mildew.'

'I did too,' Emily said, and pushed the pram across the road to the Range Rover.

It was Emily's mum Trish who wound down the window.

'What are you doing back in town?' Emily asked. 'I thought you'd gone back to Acaster Mildew.'

'Oliver relapsed,' Trish said, a tone of 'told-you-so' in her voice. 'He demanded to be brought back to York. No doubt to buy cheap bottles of cider and pass out under a tree.'

'Oh dear,' Emily said, but she did not care too much about Oliver. He had used her cat to profiteer from begging.

'Your dad has had a few glasses of wine so I thought I'd better bring him back.'

'I see.'

'Your dad said he could use the Acaster Mildew community bicycle to get back, but I said I wouldn't want a guest of ours to be seen riding the village bike. Who knows who's been on that saddle!

'And your dad said Oliver is no longer a guest of ours. He is a disappointment. He said he didn't care if he caught something fatal from the village bike.

'So I said that I would drive him back to York and your dad should have a strong cup of Yorkshire Tea. He should never have brought Oliver back to Acaster Mildew in the first place. The man is beyond hope. But you know your father. When he gets something in his head…

'So here I am. Would you like some parkin?'

'Parking?' Emily said.

'Parkin,' Trish said. 'It's traditional. On Bonfire Night.'

'Oh, parkin,' Emily said. 'No, I think I'm all right.'

'I made a batch this morning. Your father and I were going to go to the village bonfire this evening.

'Any luck finding Theo?'

Emily shook her head. 'I'm so worried.'

'It's awfully busy,' Trish said. 'All these people… There were hundreds more coming out of the station when I drove past.'

'It's an awful night,' Emily agreed.

'How about I take Joseph back to Acaster Mildew with me? You know your dad would love it. They can watch Mr Bean DVDs together. We have the car seat plugged in and ready to go.'

'Would you? That would be so kind. We could pick him up in the morning.'

'You'll need to fold up his buggy,' Trish said. 'You know I'm hopeless at that.'

Five minutes later, Joseph was strapped into his car seat, the pram folded up in the back of the car, and on the way to spend the night at his grandparents. He gurgled happily in his car seat and even managed a wave through the car window at his mum, as the car pulled away.

Emily and Jonathan entered through the gates of the Museum Gardens.

Milton wondered what had happened to the peacocks that used to live in the Museum Gardens. Then he thought of his brother Miles. No doubt he was lying low until a decent-sized crowd had gathered in front of the Minster. He would want to maximise the damage.

He shivered. His jeans were still wet from the King's Arms. He needed to get warm. He needed to build another fire.

He found some dried leaves and created a large pile. Then he went into the shrubbery and emerged minutes later, his arms laden with twigs. He placed them over the leaves and then went looking for branches. Once he had built a fire, he realised that he needed a light. He spotted some people in the distance and from the glowing orange dots, knew there were smokers among them. He approached and asked for a light.

Taking the proffered lighter, he said, 'I'll be back in a minute.'

As he was lighting the fire, the man whose lighter it was approached.

'What are you doing?'

'I'm building a fire,' Milton said.

'A bonfire?' the man said. 'What a good idea. Let me help. We'll go and get lots of wood. We'll make a massive bonfire!'

He walked back to his friends. 'We're making a massive fire!' he said. 'A bonfire! Come on! We need wood!'

Twenty feet below the ground, Theodore heard a movement behind him. He glanced back. He saw a pair of red eyes glow in the darkness. The creature had a glistening black coat and white fangs. It was a giant rat.

He began to run. The rat gave chase, its claws scratching against the stone floor behind him. It was gaining on him. Ahead of him, Theodore saw a light coming from the roof of the tunnel.

The Roman Bath

The Roman Bath is probably the only public house in the world to have a Roman bath in its basement.

During renovations to the tavern on St Sampson's Square in 1930, the remains of the Roman bath including a caldarium, or steam room, and also a plunge pool, were revealed. Two thousand years ago, Roman soldiers would come here to relax and leave cleaner than when they arrived.

Miles had ordered his meal at the bar and was sitting at a table nursing a pint and waiting for it to arrive. It was a pity that he hadn't got to eat the chicken schnitzel back at Bettys. It was a pity he had been interrupted while he was making the final preparations for this evening. It was a pity he had had to cut the American's throat and leave his body in the toilet cubicle. He'd only just managed to squeeze through the gap between the cubicle walls and the ceiling and make his escape.

He glanced at the rucksack on the floor by his feet. Then he glanced at his watch. He wanted to make sure that it had the maximum impact. He planned to wait until the crowds of protestors converged on York Minster. At nine o'clock these protestors would realise that their protests were a waste of time. Direct action would always win the day. He grinned to himself.

Miles had spent five years in prison for manipulating bank-reported interest rates, in order to enhance his own trading results; he had been sent down for ten. His brother Milton had got less time for murder. The world was truly unfair.

Five years is a long time to stare at the walls. He was separated from the other prisoners for his own protection. The guards had also taken an instant dislike to the over-educated banker, who had been rewarded more in bonuses in one year than they would in their entire unrewarding working lives.

Miles never regretted anything he had done. In his mind he had done nothing wrong, except for trusting his colleagues and managers. They didn't say anything when he was making money for them. He had done what was expected of him at the time. He had been no different to the hundreds of others working in finance and lining their pockets. Why else would you work in finance unless you wanted to make some money?

When the system finally came unstuck, he got no support from any of them. He must have had scapegoat tattooed on his forehead. They singled him out and made an example of him. It was his face on the cover of the papers.

Miles kept his head down while inside, conformed to the rules and was released on licence three months ago. His wife had already moved on, filing for divorce within months of his being put away. When he was finally released, he had nothing but a letter from the Child Support Agency setting out how much he was to pay his ex-wife for the maintenance of their three children.

That was also the time when he had got a letter from his brother asking for money. The letter went straight in the bin.

A week later he got another letter from his brother Milton. This letter also went straight in the bin. Then he had a phone call from an unknown mobile number. He answered it. It was Milton. He had somehow managed to get a mobile in prison. He asked for money again; that he wanted to take his case back to court and was going to represent himself. Miles told him what he could do. Then he told him he was coming up to York to pay a visit soon. He had his own plans for the night of the Million Mask March. Bonfire Night was going to end with a bang, he told his brother. Then he hung up.

And now his brother had somehow managed to escape from Full Sutton prison and was no doubt going to try to put a stop to his plans.

A plate of sausage, mash and peas was put down in front of him. 'There you go, love,' the barmaid said. 'Knives and forks are on the bar.'

At least he had a decent meal in front of him, he thought, thinking back to the grub back inside.

Downstairs Theodore emerged from a hole in the basement floor and stepped into the caldarium. The floor of the steam room had been removed, exposing the short stone columns that had once supported the floor. The giant rat emerged a moment later, drool hanging from its sharp fangs.

Theodore weaved between the stone columns, the rat snapping its teeth at his tail. He saw steps leading upwards. He flew up them.

He was in a crowded bar room.

Someone screamed: 'There's a stray cat!'

Someone else shouted: 'There's a giant rat!'

'I'm never eating here again,' someone muttered.

Theodore ran under a table. He was face to face with a large blue rucksack. He had seen it somewhere before. The rucksack ticked.

Then the rat was upon him. It locked its jaws onto his tail. Theodore swung around and hissed at the rat.

The man whose table they were under jumped to his feet.

The cat and the rat were battling it out on the pub floor, jaws biting into furry flesh.

Miles raised his foot and kicked out at the skirmishing animals. He caught the rat below the belly.

The rat flew through the air and landed on the bar, in front of several barstool drinkers. Stunned, it lay on a beer towel and closed its eyes.

There was shouting, screaming and cursing. People began to make their way outside to St Sampsons Square.

In the ensuing confusion, Miles picked up a sausage from his plate, popped it into his mouth like a cigar, picked up his rucksack, slung it over his shoulder and made for the door.

Theodore followed.

The Peacocks of the Museum Gardens

The peacocks of the Museum Gardens are no more.

For over seventy years they resided in the gardens: loitering in the ruins of St Mary's abbey, strutting about in the botanical gardens, screaming at people from the safety of trees, stopping the traffic on Museum Street when they decided to go for a wander down Coney Street.

In 2000 there were four birds: two males, a peahen and a chick. But the peahen decided to relocate with her chick, leaving the two males by themselves. For a peacock to be happy, he needs a harem of six peahens, so to ensure the continued presence of peacocks in the gardens, it would require a total of fourteen or fifteen birds to sustain the population.

The city was divided on the issue. Many didn't like the screaming the birds made. Many didn't like their journeys interrupted when they decided to stray onto the roads. Bus drivers didn't like it when the birds decided to hop a lift on the bus roof to visit their peacock friends in Bootham Park. Even the gardeners complained that they scratted up their plants. So it was decided after some debate that new birds would not be introduced and the remaining ones would be left to dwindle and die. It is unclear who made this final decision regarding the fate of the peacocks. They were evidently not peacock fans.

In February 2001 one of the peacocks was found dead in the gardens. The other carried on a solitary existence until 2009. On the fifth of November, the local paper reported that the last peacock had died.

That is what happened to the peacocks of the Museum Gardens.

Milton wished they were still there. They had brought colour to the gardens even in the middle of winter. When he was a teenager, drinking cider in the bushes, he would listen to them calling out to each other in the darkness, and he would copy them, calling out, 'Bu-kirk! Bu-kirk!' It had made him feel better.

He looked into the flames of the fire he had built and screamed, 'Bu-kirk! Bu-kirk!'

Some younger people who were standing by his fire backed away from him and made their way back into the darkness.

'We need a guy,' a man said.

Milton turned to his companion. It was the same man who had helped him collect firewood.

'A guy?' Milton said.

'You know… A penny for the guy and all that. A figure to burn on the fire. We should make a guy and then parade it through the streets. We might make a bit of money.'

'There will be no guy on this bonfire,' Milton said, staring into the flames.

Milton had attended St Peter's School on Bootham until his A Levels, when his father had refused to carry on with the cost and then ended up under a bus. It was St Peter's policy not to burn a guy on their annual bonfire as Guy Fawkes had gone to St Peter's some four hundred years earlier. It is usually not a good school policy to burn effigies of your former pupils on bonfires each year.

Milton stared into the flames, remembering. 'Remember, remember…' he murmured, 'the fifth of November.'

'A toast!' Sylvia slurred from her sofa, her Dachshund Dolly on her lap. 'A toast for my big boy!' Both Milton and Miles referred to the worn pink chaise longue as 'her sofa', as their mother spent most of her waking as well as sleeping hours on it, either sprawled out watching television or sitting up reading *Hello* magazines.

Milton took a sip of tea. He had always been an avid tea drinker. And he knew that Yorkshire Tea was the best.

Sylvia, undeterred, raised her glass in the air. Dolly squirmed to her paws and jumped down from the chaise longue. Miles raised a can of lager to his lips.

'I can't believe you're going off to university,' Sylvia said. 'It only seems like yesterday that I was bottle feeding you, right here on the sofa.'

She patted the seat beside her and managed to spill some wine on the upholstery. Dolly scampered under the sofa.

Milton noticed several dark brown chipolatas on the parquet floor beneath the sofa. Dolly needed to be let out more often, he thought. He looked across at his brother. It was three weeks since they had seen their father put into the ground.

Miles was pacing up and down, distracted. He was taking a train down to London the next day. His mother didn't drive, so he had little choice in the matter.

'I'll have to come down and visit one weekend,' Milton said. It was his attempt at making the peace; he doubted he would ever go and visit; he had never been to London.

'I don't think so,' Miles said.

'Don't be like that, Miles,' Sylvia said. 'Not on your last night at home.'

She got up and went into the kitchen to pour herself another glass of wine.

'I meant it,' Miles said. 'I never want to see you or her again.'

'Whatever,' Milton said. He shrugged.

'You don't get it,' do you? Miles said.

'What's that?'

'Don't you see? You're ginger…'

'So?'

'Did you not do biology in school?'

Miles took a drink of beer and stared out of the window, at the house opposite. 'The Ginger Ferret… That's what dad used to call him.'

Milton was confused. 'Who's this Ginger Ferret?'

'He was the neighbour,' Miles said. 'He upped and left. You're not one of us.'

Sylvia came back into the lounge.

'Now, where were we?' she said. 'A toast! That's right. A toast to my son. A toast to my big boy!'

Miles stood up. 'Oh, do be quiet,' he said. 'I'm going to bed.'

'But it's not even nine.'

'I've had enough,' Miles said. 'Of you. Of him. Of this house. I'm going to bed now.' Then he went upstairs.

Milton sipped his tea. His mother would be dead by Christmas. He would be seventeen and left to live on his own in that awful house. He would never sit on her sofa though. It was left like a forgotten museum piece.

Twenty five years later, he stared into the flames of the bonfire. The fire was dying down. He was going to have to find some more firewood. He turned his back to the fire and made his way over to some trees.

'Do you really think he might be in here?' Emily asked.

'If I were a cat,' Jonathan said, 'it's where I'd go. Somewhere dark and out of the way. The less people, the better.'

A firework went off with a bang and the sky was momentarily lit up with white light.

'It's very smoky,' Emily said.

'There must be a fire.'

'In the gardens?'

'Somebody must have started a fire. A bonfire… It'll be one of the protestors. Come on. We need to look in the bushes. That's where I'd hide. In the darkest places.'

Jonathan headed off towards some dark shrubbery. Emily followed.

It was only once Jonathan had entered the shrubs did he realise he was not alone. A man was stooping down, picking up sticks. His arms full the man turned and came towards Jonathan. It was only when he was almost on top of him did the man see him.

He was wearing a Guy Fawkes mask pushed back on top of his head, an old army coat, a red and black checked shirt and jeans that were too short for him.

Jonathan recognised the man from the news that morning. He also recognised his shirt and jeans.

'I know who you are,' he said. 'You're Milton Macavity.'

'That's my name,' Milton said. 'Don't wear it out.'

Milton moved to the side to step around Jonathan.

'Not so fast,' Jonathan said. 'I'm making a citizen's arrest.'

Milton shook his head, looked Jonathan up and down. 'Well, well, well. Who do we have here? The Corduroy Kid…?'

Jonathan looked down at his clothes. He was dressed entirely in beige corduroy. When he had returned home to check for Theodore, he had taken off his denim jacket which was soaked through with rain. When he had left home again to rejoin Emily he had put on his corduroy jacket, not realising he was doubling up on the corduroy.

Suddenly he was angry that his fashion faux pas had been called out by this escaped convict.

'You're right,' he shouted. 'I'm the Corduroy Kid and you're under arrest!'

Milton laughed. He dropped his pile of firewood. Then he punched Jonathan in the nose.

Emily screamed.

Jonathan dropped to his knees, blood spilling down his corduroy jacket.

Milton pushed his way past. 'Nice meeting you,' he called out, disappearing into the smoky night.

'I can't believe how bad this day is turning out,' Jonathan said.

'Well, we all have our sartorial mishaps,' Emily said, crouching down beside him. 'I was going to point it out earlier but I was more concerned about Theodore.'

'I meant being punched in the face by an escaped convict.'

'You mean that was Milton Macavity?'

'Yes,' Jonathan said. 'And he was wearing my shirt and jeans, I'm sure of it.'

'We need to find the police and let them know,' Emily said. 'They need to catch him… Then you can get your clothes back. We can't have you going around in double corduroy, can we?'

A Penny for the Percy

There was a huge explosion. Then the sky lit up green. Then a high-pitched whizzing went overhead. A star exploded, pink and green. Then came a volley of short sharp bangs, like machine gun fire. It was as though Theodore was caught up in the middle of a warzone.

Whoever invented fireworks should have a rocket inserted up their rectum, Theodore thought, flicking his tail from side to side.

He carried on down Low Petergate. There were many shop signs hanging over the crowded street. One sign read: 'The Cat Gallery'. I didn't know cats could paint, he thought. We cats are a species of many talents.

He turned left into Stonegate and spotted the bulky rucksack passing through the crowd. He dashed after it, giving a purple man on a purple bicycle a wide berth.

The man in mauve was a living statue, who made his living by posing as a windswept cyclist on Stonegate. He also collected money for charity. His mission was to spread love and happiness throughout the world. He had been to war-torn Syria, where he had handed out a thousand soft toys to the surprised children. They were surprised to see him as they had never seen a purple man before.

Miles stopped and Theodore stopped.

Miles was staring down at a crumpled, dirt-streaked Guy Fawkes mask, lying in the gutter. He picked the mask up. There was a warning sticker inside. 'Keep Away From Fire,' it read.

A man wearing the same style Guy Fawkes mask approached.

'They're selling them on Coney Street for a tenner if you want one,' the man said.

Miles stared at the masked face. 'What do you know about Fawkes?'

'They're cutlery, aren't they?'

'Fawkes... Guy Fawkes,' Miles said.

'That Fawkes,' the man in the mask said, who happened to be studying seventeenth century history at York University. 'Well, he was born around here, someplace. He went to St Peter's School in Bootham. His father died when he was a teenager. Guy was executed outside Westminster, the place they had planned to blow up rather ironically, on the thirtieth of January 1606...'

'He was a scapegoat,' Miles cut in.

'He was responsible for placing the gunpowder and guarding it. He was culpable.'

'He was just one of thirteen conspirators. It was Thomas Percy who funded it. Catesby and Percy were the ones behind the scheme. Fawkes was just employed because of his military background. His knowledge of explosives.'

'Well, why don't we hear more about this Percy?'

'Well,' Miles said, deliberating. 'It doesn't have the same ring, does it? "A penny for the Percy." "Let's put a Percy on the bonfire."'

'I wouldn't want my Percy burning on a fire.'

'This is not a joking matter,' Miles went on. 'When arrested, Guy Fawkes claimed he was John Johnson, servant of Thomas Percy... It was Percy who had put him up to it. It was Percy who had financed the plot. It was Percy's name which appeared first on the arrest warrant.'

'So what happened to this Percy?'

'Percy fled to the Midlands where he met up with Catesby. They engaged with government forces and, they say, Percy and Catesby were killed by the same musket ball. They were buried but later exhumed, so that their heads could be put on spikes outside of Parliament. They got off lightly…'

'So why do we only hear about Guy Fawkes then?'

'Fawkes was tortured. His torture was so cruel that he could hardly sign his name to his supposed confession.'

'The Attorney General told the court that each of the condemned would be "put to death halfway between heaven and earth as unworthy of both. Their genitals would be cut off and burnt before their eyes, and their bowels and hearts removed. They would then be decapitated, and the dismembered parts of their bodies displayed so that they might become prey for the fowls of the air…"

'So, on the last day of January 1606, Fawkes and his fellow plotters were dragged from the Tower to the Old Palace Yard at Westminster. Fawkes was the last to be sent to the scaffold. Weak from torture, he was helped by the hangman to climb the ladder to the noose. He managed to climb so high that the drop broke his neck, and he was saved the agonies promised him. He was taken down, quartered and his body parts sent out to the four corners of the kingdom…'

For Fawkes' sake, thought Theodore. This is turning into a horrible history lesson.

Theodore, like many cats, was not keen on history. In fact it had been his worst subject at school.

Then he felt hands tighten around him.

The Good Samaritan

'I've got him,' Becky said. 'It's that cat that's missing. I saw it on Facebook.'

'Looks like a street cat to me,' her friend Sam said.

Sam backed into a shop doorway, still clutching the cat. 'I'm sure it's him. His name's Theodore.'

'He doesn't have a collar on,' Sam said. 'Just put him back down. You can tell he doesn't want to be picked up.'

Theodore struggled in Becky's grasp. His manhunt had been halted by millennials. Excuse me, he thought, but I have the important business of catching escaped convicts and crooked bankers who would prefer you dead.

'Just leave him be,' Sam said. 'He'll find his own way home.

'This woman on Facebook was really worried,' Becky said. 'What with it being Bonfire Night and all. Pets shouldn't be allowed out. I need to contact her.'

'But we're missing the protest. And I heard that there's going to be a gig in the gardens later on. There's a rumour that Radiohead are flying over from America to play just one gig and then fly back tomorrow, just to highlight the threat from climate change…'

'Then the sooner we get Theodore returned to his owner the better. Here you hold him and I'll find the post on Facebook. She's probably in town somewhere looking for him.'

Becky passed the cat to Sam.

Her day had not gone well. When she had arrived at the shoe shop on Pavement that morning, she found out that the shop was due to close. Herbert House was to close for renovation and the shop's lease was not being renewed. She had been manhandled by escaped convict Milton Macavity in the alley behind the shop. She had then had to go with the police to Fulford Police Station, where she had made a statement.

She had told the police what Milton had said to her about there being some terrible plot for that evening and his brother being behind it, but the police hadn't seemed to take it too seriously. The escaped convict was trying to take attention away from himself and what better way than to claim there was going to be some form of terrorist plot planned for the centre of York. They probably had a point, she'd thought, once she had managed to get home.

'This protest is a bit of a let-down anyway,' Becky said. 'I mean there aren't even any TV cameras. If it's not on the telly, there's no point in doing it, is there? We need exposure.'

'But we have to make a stand now,' Sam said, taking Theodore. 'Before it's too late. There is no Planet B, remember?'

Becky was wearing a T-shirt that read, 'There is no Planet B.' It showed a forlorn polar bear heading towards a pine forest, a mountain range in the background.

Theodore struggled in the hands of his new captor.

Sam held onto him, pulling him tightly against her chest. Her T-shirt read, 'Help More Bees. Plant More Trees. Clean The Seas.'

Get Off, Please, thought Theodore, still struggling.

He understood that the two young women were trying to help reunite him with Emily. Unfortunately they were impeding his attempts to stop Miles.

Becky took out her mobile and opened Facebook. She searched her groups until she found the 'Pets – Lost & Found – York-UK' group. She scrolled down until she found Emily's post.

'I think we've found your cat,' she wrote. 'We're outside the Teddy Bear Shop on Stonegate. Please come quickly! Not sure how long we can hold onto him…'

'You take him back,' Sam said. 'I don't think I can hold onto him much longer.'

She passed the struggling cat back to Becky. Becky slipped her mobile into her jeans pocket and then took Theodore. She held him with both hands so that he faced away from her, his hind legs dangling down.

'We'll be missing the speeches,' Sam said.

'We can't let him go though,' Becky said. 'He's scared out of his mind. We need to do the right thing. We need to reunite him with his owner.'

Emily and Jonathan made their way back to the entrance of the Museum Gardens. More protestors were entering the gardens and they had to make their way against the flow.

'I need to get home and lie down on the sofa,' Jonathan said, holding his nose between two fingers to stem the bleeding.'

'You can go and lie on the sofa,' Emily said. 'I'm not going to return without Theodore.'

By the entrance someone was handing out flyers. Jonathan waved one away when it was pushed towards him.

Emily felt her phone vibrate in her pocket. She backed up against a wall and clicked on the alert.

'Someone's found Theodore,' she said. 'He's at the Teddy Bear Shop on Stonegate.'

She texted, 'I'm on my way. Five minutes max. Please don't let go of him.'

Then she said to Jonathan, 'Come on. We're going to get Theodore.'

And she pushed through the crowd on Museum Street.

Becky felt her mobile pulse in the back of her jeans.

'Sam. Get my phone from my back pocket. I think she might have responded to my message.'

Sam took Becky's mobile. 'You have an alert,' she said. 'She's responded. She's on her way.'

Looks like you're coming home whether you like it or not, came the voice of the cat basket. *Your little adventure is at an end. I'll be seeing you soon no doubt. Then we can get reacquainted…*

It's not over 'til the fat cat miaows, thought Theodore. He kicked backwards with his hind legs, catching Becky in the stomach with his claws.

'That hurt,' she gasped, but she did not let go. 'Your owner is on her way. Just stay still, will you?'

Theodore stared out into the crowd, expecting to see Emily approach. But instead he saw Miles with his bulky blue rucksack hurry past.

He kicked out with his legs again but this time Becky pulled her body backwards and managed to avoid his claws.

He glanced from side to side. He spied some flesh on her arm that he could just about reach. He twisted in her grasp.

This is going to hurt you more than it's going to hurt me, he thought. Then he twisted to one side and bit Becky on the arm.

She cried out in pain and dropped Theodore to the ground. She looked at her arm that was bleeding just above the wrist.

'This is turning out to be the worst day of my life,' she said, staring after Theodore's grey tail as the cat disappeared into the crowd.

The End of Purpleman

Milton knew he had to return to the crowded streets and find Miles, before his brother could carry out whatever fiendish act he had in mind.

He pushed his way through a large group of people at the entrance to the Museum Gardens. He noticed some protestors lying down in the road in front of Pizza Express, stopping the traffic from passing through the city. Police officers stood by the protestors. Car drivers blew their horns in frustration. Milton watched on as a police officer stopped a taxi driver from dragging a Radiohead fan from the road.

He stared at the crowd for his brother. There were so many masked faces. There were those in Guy Fawkes masks. Then there was a smaller group of people wearing cow masks, their black clothes daubed with white paint, so that they resembled Friesian cows. They carried a banner that read, 'Dairy is Scary!' Then there were people wearing badger masks and also dressed in black and white. They carried a banner that read, 'Innocent Till Proven Guilty!'

His brother may well have got a mask. He might even be dressed as a cow or badger. He shrugged his shoulders in despair; perhaps he should have stayed put in prison.

Then he remembered his brother had been carrying a rucksack. A large bulky rucksack. He needed to find the rucksack and his brother.

He turned, pulled his Guy Fawkes mask down and set off towards the Minster. That was where most of the crowd seemed to be drifting. That would be where Miles was heading.

As he walked, he remembered the last time he had seen his brother.

He had caught the National Express down to London. His trial was coming to a close and he was about to be sentenced.

On the coach, he noticed other travellers reading tabloids. His brother's face was on many of the front pages. The headlines read:

DISGRACED FINANCIER
BANKER WANKERED
GREEDY SWINE
TIME TO PAY THE PRICE

The general public had no sympathy for the former banker. Scapegoat or not, he epitomised the hated public-school-educated City types who received massive bonuses while they worked long hours for little reward.

Outside the court, Milton watched from the crowd of onlookers as Miles was brought out. His eyes darted among the crowd.

'Miles!' a woman shouted.

Milton looked across and saw Carol, Miles's wife. Milton had never met Carol Macavity but he recognised her from photographs in the newspapers. Miles's former personal assistant and then trophy wife.

'Carol?' Miles said, uncertainty in his voice.

The crowd quietened down, suspecting some outburst of emotion. Cameras flashed. Television cameras turned from husband to wife and back again.

'I'm divorcing you!' Carol cried in a Cockney accent. 'And I'm going to take you for every penny you own.'

A cheer went up from the crowd.

'You're finished,' she went on. 'I'll make sure of it!'

Miles didn't respond. He let himself be led to the waiting Amey van.

As he passed, Milton called out, 'I'll write to you!'

Miles turned and caught his brother's eye. 'Don't bother,' he called back.

Some of the crowd had begun to chant, 'Wanker Banker! Wanker Banker! Wanker Banker!'

Milton watched as the van doors were closed; then he turned and began to walk back to Victoria Coach Station. Miles was the only family he had in the world. But then if what Miles had implied was true, they were only half-brothers. His own father was a ginger-haired former neighbour he had never known. He felt very alone as he walked along the crowded streets of the Big Smoke.

Milton was brought back to the present with a jolt. Someone had shoved him as they passed by. He looked up and saw a man with a big blue rucksack pushing his way through the crowd. It was Miles. Milton started after him.

Miles was making his way down Stonegate towards York Minster, the rucksack on his back.

He glanced at the faces of the young people around him, in their T-shirts with slogans and cheap plastic masks.

It is easy to be idealistic when you are young, he thought. These kids would have it kicked out of them before too long.

By his forties, Miles had already spent twenty years in the dog-eat-dog world of finance. It was trample or be trampled on.

The traders were known as fat cats but they were more like feral cats, fighting over the meagre scraps dropped from the dining table of the top cats, the few who really ran everything.

Under his breath he quoted:

> *'Remember, remember the fifth of November,*
> *Gunpowder treason and plot.*
> *We see no reason*
> *Why gunpowder treason*
> *Should ever be forgot!'*

He pulled on the straps of the rucksack. There was quite a weight in the bag. I'm going to give you a fifth of November to remember!

Then he heard a shout from behind him. He turned and saw a man wearing a Guy Fawkes mask coming straight at him.

'Miles!' Milton shouted. 'Stop there!'

Miles turned back round but he didn't stop. He carried on, past the purple man on his purple bike. He pushed people aside, shouting at them to get out of his way. The crowd parted, pushing themselves to the sides of the street.

Milton saw the purple man on his purple bike. One of those living statues, he thought. Another person trying to make a living by not doing much of anything.

He pushed the purple man off his bike. A purple pot of coins crashed onto the pavement; silver and gold coins spilled out onto the flagstones. The bike fell to the ground. Milton snatched it up. He would soon catch up with his brother on this purple bike.

He jumped on it and pressed the pedals. But they did not turn.

'Bloody useless thing! he shouted, as Miles turned a corner and disappeared from sight.

'It's a prop!' Purpleman shouted from the ground.

Two men approached. They were dressed in black shirts and trousers but wore purple ties.

They were security guards employed by Purpleman to protect him from drunken racegoers, stag and hen parties and football fans. It wasn't the first time that Purpleman had been pushed off his bike.

One of the security guards helped Purpleman to his feet; the other turned to Milton. 'What do you think you're playing at?'

'I needed to borrow a bike…'

Milton threw the bike back onto the ground. 'It's bloody useless…' A purple toy dog fell from its purple basket at the front of the bike.

'I know you,' the security guard said. 'You're Milton Macavity… The so-called Napoleon of Crime. Been reduced to stealing bikes, have you?'

Milton raised his hands to his face. Somehow he had lost his Guy Fawkes mask.

The security guard had a walkie-talkie. 'Come in, come in,' he said. 'I'm going to need some assistance.'

Purpleman replaced his purple hat which had a small purple camera mounted on the top. 'I've had enough!' he shouted. 'I've been sworn at, spat at… had things thrown at me. I've been pushed off my bike. I've had enough.'

'Sorry,' Milton said.

'Sorry?' Purpleman said. 'You're sorry? I have tried to bring some love and laughter to this city. I have tried to bring out the awesomeness in everyone. But look at them.' He waved his hands dramatically at the crowd around him. 'All I see is hatred. I have failed in my mission. Now I am going home. I quit… No longer will Purpleman be the object of ridicule. No longer will he bring smiles to the faces of those both young and old. I am going home.'

Purpleman threw his purple hat onto the ground and then walked away. The crowd stood in silence, knowing that they would never see him again and that they were partly to blame.

Milton watched as Purpleman disappeared into the crowd. He then turned and began to make his way in the opposite direction, after Miles. But a hand grabbed his shoulder and spun him round.

'You're not going anywhere,' one of the security guards said. 'There's a police van on its way. You're going back inside…'

'You don't understand,' Milton said. 'There's a plot to blow up the Minster. My brother Miles is behind it. We need to stop him.'

'You want us to believe that?' The security guard laughed. 'You're going back inside, mate.'

The other security guard approached. On his jacket he wore insignia that read, 'Eboracum Security'. 'Not such a big shot, are we now?'

Milton pushed the security guard squarely in the chest so that he fell against his partner. Then he spun round and began to run.

A York Ghost Story

Theodore followed Miles into the crowd that was heading towards the Minster. The shoes and boots drew ever tighter around him. He slipped between the protestors, dodging footwear from all sides while trying to keep sight of the blue rucksack as it moved through the crowd. But soon the rucksack disappeared.

He kept to the side of a pub. At cat's eye level, he read:

'IT WAS HERE I WAS BORN.
IT IS HERE WHERE THEY SERVE
THE BEST PIE IN THE CITY OF YORK.'
GUY FAWKES

I may well have to head back there and sample one of these pies, Theodore thought, once I have stopped Miles carrying out whatever heinous deed he has set his heart on.

He noted that the pub was unimaginatively called the Guy Fawkes Inn, for it was here that Fawkes is reported to have been born in 1570, in the shadow of York Minster and across the street from the church where he was baptised, St Michael Le Belfrey.

Ahead of him, Theodore spotted a very tall man wearing a top hat standing on the lawn off College Street. He must have been ten feet tall. In front of the very tall man there was a large crowd. He must be wearing some contraptions on his legs to be so tall, Theodore realised.

Theodore spied Oliver Bartholomew leaning against the trunk of a large tree in the shadow of York Minster. In his hand he had a two litre bottle of cider. Theodore slipped among the crowd gathered in front of the very tall man. He didn't want to be snatched by Oliver again.

People were packed tightly around him. He spotted a raised plinth about two feet above the ground. He jumped up on top of the bronze plinth.

A plan of York Minster was portrayed on the plinth. Theodore padded across a bright red circle that had 'YOU ARE HERE,' written below it. The red circle had an aureole of shiny metal around it from people putting their finger on it.

Theodore entered the Minster from the east end. He passed by the entrance to the crypt and the quire, before settling down in the nave, his tail extending into the south transept of the largest Gothic cathedral in northern Europe. I never realised I was so big, thought Theodore, to be able to fill the nave of York Minster.

The tall man in the top hat began to tell a story, a ghost story.

'Some sixty years ago,' the top-hatted man began, 'a family moved into the house over there. They had acquired it at a bargain price. A house in the shadows of the Minster… Usually they don't come cheap.

'But they were not aware of the house's horrible history…' The man paused for dramatic effect.

Not another horrible history, thought Theodore.

'Weeks after they had moved in,' the man continued, 'strange things began to happen. The parents heard the wails of a young girl. When they went to their children's bedroom, they found them wide awake, the light in their bedroom turned on. They asked them what the matter was…

'The children said that they had seen a young girl sitting at the foot of the bed. When they had turned the light on, the girl was gone. The children refused to sleep in the room.

'The next day the parents began to ask questions…

'They discovered that during the plague, a husband and wife and their daughter had lived in the house. Both the husband and wife had contracted the disease. They were sealed in their house, so as to stop the spread of the disease within the city; their doors and windows were nailed shut. They quickly succumbed to pestilence. They were fortunate. Their daughter was not so fortunate.' Again the tall man paused for dramatic effect.

'Unfortunately for her, she was immune to the disease…

'With her parents lying dead in the next room, she tapped at her little window, trying to get the attention of those passing on the road outside. She saw the carts of corpses being drawn by, being carried to the pits where they were covered in lime. She called and called at the passing people. But the people ignored her cries. They were worried that if she were released, she would infect them. During times of plague, there is little time for compassion.

'So, without food or water, she eventually died. But, as you know, the human spirit does not give in easily. For weeks she fought death. Eventually she succumbed. When death did finally come, it was a blessing…

'The house is now occupied by another family,' the tall man said. 'They do not believe in ghosts…'

The man turned and pointed at a small rectangular window set into a limestone block wall. 'In that window, some people claim that they have seen the girl's face. And on quiet nights, some people claim that they have heard the girl's cries.'

The man paused and the crowd stared at the small window. A silent minute passed.

'Now, we will make our way to our next haunted location. Please follow closely behind. York is very busy tonight… I wouldn't want to lose any of you.'

As the crowd followed the top-hatted man on stilts towards their next haunted location, Theodore stared up at the window.

Suddenly a girl's face appeared. Then he heard a wailing noise, a young girl crying out within the prison of her house.

He glanced around him. Oliver was still leaning against the tree. He was staring wide-eyed at the small window.

Oliver shook his head in disbelief. He lifted his bottle of cider to his mouth with both hands and took a big gulp. Then he staggered off towards the Minster, his head bowed.

Theodore watched him depart. Then he looked back up at the little window. He didn't believe in ghost stories. He knew they were based on human superstition and had their roots in the humans' misunderstanding of the world. There was always a feline explanation to most things, he knew.

He heard a peel of laugher and then excited voices. He looked back up at the little window.

He saw the young girl's face staring out into the night. Then it was joined by the face of a young boy. They were both giggling.

'Did you see that silly man,' the boy said.

'Yes,' the young girl said, 'he fell for it, hook line and sinker!'

'We really put the wind up him!'

And both the children laughed.

Theodore blinked. I told you that there would be a simple explanation, he thought. Then he set off after Oliver Bartholomew towards the Minster.

Bovine vs Badger

The war between the bovine and the badgers had been going on for many centuries.

It was a distant memory to both creatures when they had peacefully shared the British countryside; before the humans had sided with the cows, understanding that they could be cultivated for food on a commercial scale while the badgers were harder to catch and didn't taste as good.

The badgers were driven to ever-diminishing areas of woodland, as the land was given over to the ever-increasing herds of cattle. The dominant cows were mostly ambivalent about the matter; many of them did not even know there was a war: they spent so much time munching grass and farting clouds of methane that they had little time to think.

Sensing defeat, the badgers resorted to biological warfare: spreading bovine tuberculosis among the herds of cows.

The cows launched a propaganda war in response: Rumours abound that they were using their methane farts like napalm, wiping out huge areas of the remaining woodland indiscriminately. But on hearing this false news, the badgers knew it was just bullshit.

Then the humans got wind of the badger fightback and intervened, culling badgers in Gloucestershire and Somerset. The badgers retaliated, laying siege to Stroud with a network of sinkholes, resulting in a nationwide shortage of green baize for covering snooker tables and tennis balls. (The manufacture of baize is one of

Stroud's few remaining industries, along with organic banana cake and Damien Hirst artworks).

Some humans sided with the badgers. They tended to be people who didn't like the idea of trained marksmen shooting down our remaining wild animals. Their numbers included many veterinarian surgeons, many of whom were veterans of the Stroud offensive. They called themselves the Badger Protection Squad, or the BPS for short.

Others sided with the cows. They tended to be those who enjoyed eating steaks and drinking milk. Their numbers included many snooker players and tennis fans. They called themselves the Bovine Preservation Society, or the BPS for short.

There were also cow supporters who didn't enjoy steaks or milk; they objected to the treatment of the cows by the human farmers. But they quite liked badgers too, so were undecided when it came down to which BPS to support.

So, on this Bonfire Night, the warring BPS factions met in front of York Minster. It wasn't long before skirmishes broke out between those dressed as cows and those dressed as badgers.

In the middle of the melee, a cow furry faced off a badger furry. The cow furry was flanked by angry snooker players and tennis fans wielding snooker cues and tennis rackets. The badger furry was flanked by angry vets, sporting elbow length gloves.

'You disease-ridden creature,' the cow furry shouted at the badger furry. 'You should all be stood in front of a wall and shot!'

'You're full of hot air,' the badger furry shouted back. 'Get back to eating grass and farting in your field.'

'At least I don't root about in the dirt and eat worms and slugs...'

'At least I don't have suction cups stuck on my tits and my milk sucked out.'

'You've gone too far with that one,' the cow furry said, coming at the badger furry, her hooves raised.

The badger furry pushed the cow furry back. The cow furry responded with a swipe of her fluffy hoof to the badger furry's black and white striped head. The badger furry jabbed the cow furry in the belly with his clawed paw. The cow furry doubled up. Other furries piled in. Scuffles broke out between the snooker players, tennis fans and elbow-length-glove-wearing vets.

The York mounted police decided to intervene. They had been armed with police-issue water blasters in case of just such an event. They knew that furries didn't like to get their fur wet.

They rode into the centre of the crowd and pulled out their water blasters. Some of the protestors stopped skirmishing. They stared at the mounted police carrying firearms. Some stood their ground; others slunk off into the shadows, not wanting to get wet. Then someone threw a banger. It went off at the horses' feet, scaring the animals.

'Right,' Paul said, 'let them have it.'

Maria pulled the trigger on her water blaster. 'Take that!' she cried. A spurt of water shot out and hit a cow supporter in the face.

Paul sprayed a group of retreating badger supporters. He laughed and then jetted more water over the crowd.

'Hey!' one Radiohead fan, who had until recently been lying on Lendal Bridge stopping traffic, shouted, 'Lay off, pig!'

One BPS member removed her cow mask and wiped the water from her eyes. She noticed that the black paint had started to flake away from the water blasters, revealing garish yellow, orange and blue plastic underneath. She turned to the crowd, who were rapidly dispersing.

'Hang on,' she shouted. 'They're just water pistols. They're not real guns... They're just Nerf water blasters, painted black.'

Paul examined his water blaster. It was true: they were just cheap, plastic water shooters, painted over with black gloss paint. 'Bloody cutbacks,' he muttered.

The crowd had started to regather. They began to surround the two mounted officers.

Maria aimed her water blaster and tried to soak a girl dressed as a badger. The badger girl laughed at her. Maria sprayed over the crowd that were closing in on them. The water pressure began to go.

'I think I'm running out of water,' she said, panicking.

'Me too... Come on, let's get out of here! Leave them to it!'

'Yes,' Maria said. 'Let's get back to the station and have a nice cup of Yorkshire Tea!'

Theodore watched as the mounted police cantered off into the night, horse hooves clipping on the flags of Yorkstone.

He was crouched at the base of the statue of Constantine the Great, located by the southern entrance to the Minster. He stared out at the crowd of masked protestors from between the great man's legs. He spotted a police dog, a German shepherd, running amok among the crowd, its handler nowhere to be seen.

Then, from the direction of Minster Yard, Miles appeared, his rucksack strapped to his back. Then, from the direction of Minster Gates, Milton appeared. Such convenient synchronicity, thought Theodore.

The two brothers saw each other at the same time. Milton headed straight for Miles. Miles ran behind the Roman Column. When he emerged seconds later, Theodore noticed that he was without his rucksack.

Theodore remembered Miles fiddling with the rucksack when he had been sitting in Pavement. Then in Bettys toilets, the rucksack had ticked three times as the door closed behind him. There had to be a bomb in the rucksack, he realised.

Miles began to push his way through the crowd, away from his younger brother. But Milton caught up with him and grabbed him by the shoulder, swinging him round.

'You're too late,' Miles cried.

Milton removed his Guy Fawkes mask. 'You what?'

'You heard,' Miles said. 'You're too late!'

Miles then hit Milton in the face. Milton staggered backwards and fell to his knees. The crowd parted around the fighting men. Milton got to his feet and the two brothers squared up.

Theodore looked across at the Roman Column. Miles must have put his rucksack behind the huge column. The bomb might go off at any minute. The explosion would cause the column to topple onto the crowd in front of the Minster, flattening the protestors.

He looked back at Miles and Milton. Milton punched his brother in the face. Blood spurted down Miles's shirt. Miles wiped the blood from his mouth and then kneed his brother in the groin. Milton doubled up in pain.

Then Theodore heard a bark. It was the police dog that had got loose. It had picked up his scent and was circling the great stone plinth on which Theodore was standing.

Theodore glanced at the Roman Column, back to the brawling brothers and then down at the barking dog.

How was he going to get off this statue and through the crowd to the column to defuse the bomb before it went off, killing and maiming innocent people?

Then he remembered the police on their horses and had an idea.

He stared down at the police dog as it did another lap of the statue. Then he approached the edge of the stone plinth. The dog did one more lap.

Theodore chose his moment. He dropped from the plinth, as the dog came round again.

Oliver Bartholomew's Last Drink

The Roman Column is subject to much misconception.

Many believe that the ancient column has stood in its current location for centuries. They are wrong. The huge erection of rock was put up in the Minster Yard in 1971, having been found in a crypt beneath the south transept of the Minster, lying where it had fallen. Originally it was built by the Ninth Legion in circa 100AD to form the north-eastern colonnade of the Roman headquarters. It was taken down and reconstructed in the fourth century.

Oliver was leaning against the ancient stone column; he liked to have something to lean against. He took a swig from his bottle of cider and gazed out dreamily at the crowd. He wasn't sure what all these people in masks and costumes were doing in front of the Minster and didn't really care about finding out. He was enjoying the fireworks that went off over the crowd every few minutes, the coloured flares of light blurring into the night sky.

Then the crowd before him suddenly parted and a cat riding on the back of a German shepherd appeared. It was the same cat he had been begging with earlier that day.

'It can't be!' he muttered.

The dog-mounted cat was heading straight for him.

'Please no!'

It was coming for its revenge.

Oliver glanced at his bottle of cider and then at the advancing cat. The dog barked, the cat wailed and

Oliver fell backwards onto the stone flags with a scream. His last thought before he blacked out: I never knew justice would take the form of a big fluffy cat riding a devil dog.

When he woke in a hospital ward the next day, he vowed never to take another drink, and the Theodore 'treatment' he had received would prove effective. The reformed Oliver Bartholomew would never have another drink in his life. After that Bonfire Night, he would be completely teetotal.

Fifty yards away, the Macavity brothers were still fighting. As anyone who has been in a fight will tell you, punching and taking punches is tiring. They stood bent over, their hands on their thighs, trying to get their breath back.

'Isn't that Milton Macavity?' one of the protestors said. 'The escaped convict?'

'And isn't that Miles Macavity?' another protestor said. 'The disgraced banker?'

'Bloody scum! Let's get them!'

And the crowd descended on the two brothers.

Theodore stared down at the ticking rucksack. He had managed to dismount his steed by the Roman Column, the dog returning to the crowd, its job done.

Theodore used his paws to lift the flap on the rucksack. There was a drawstring with a toggle attached. Theodore bit into the toggle and pulled it down the string. He then loosened the opening at the top of the bag before peering inside.

The ticking box inside was covered by many brightly coloured wires: red, green, blue and yellow. There was an LED, which ticked down the seconds until the bomb went off: 058, 057, 056, 055…

He realised that he had less than a minute to defuse the bomb. He flexed his claws and stared at the many wires and cables.

047, 046, 045, 044…

He knew that if he chose the wrong one, he would be cremains.

033, 032, 031, 029…

He thought briefly of Emily; he would never see his human ever again.

021, 020, 019, 018…

He wondered at the state of his food bowls; he would not be around to find out.

013, 012, 011…

He needed to focus on the situation. He stared at the network of wires and cables. Then he reached in a claw.

007, 006, 005…

Red, green, blue or yellow?

He reached inside.

003, 002…

He grabbed several cables in his claw and clamped down his jaws.

001…

The LED flashed 000.

Nothing happened. No big bang. No toppling column. No flattened protestors. No screaming people. Just the absence of ticking.

Theodore had saved hundreds of lives. He was a hero. Then he felt a jab in his side. He pulled his head out of the rucksack.

'Out of it!' a man in a Guy Fawkes mask said, and tapped him in his side again with his boot.

Theodore hissed at the masked man.

The man raised his foot. 'Get out of it!' he said. 'I'm having that bag and whatever's in it.'

Then Theodore was pushed aside and the masked man grabbed the rucksack. He didn't bother looking inside. He pulled it over his shoulder and disappeared into the night.

Theodore watched as the rucksack disappeared.

Now you can come home, came the voice in his head. *You managed to stop Miles killing the protestors. Your job is done. You* are *a hero! You can come back and have a long rest now.*

I will, Theodore thought back.

You will?

Yes, as soon as I've found Milton. I need to make sure he is returned safely to Full Sutton. We can't have him left wandering the streets.

Oh, please yourself, you foolish cat!

The Bonfire of the Macavities

Emily and Jonathan watched as Miles and then Milton Macavity were dragged by the angry mob through the Museum Gardens, where a big bonfire awaited the brothers.

'Well, I guess those two are going to get what's coming to them,' Emily said.

'They can't throw them on the fire,' Jonathan said.

'Why ever not?'

'Milton's got my jeans and shirt for a start,' Jonathan said, shaking his head.

'Well, maybe it's time you got yourself a new wardrobe,' Emily said. 'The Corduroy Kid!'

'Don't you start.'

'Isn't that Brian May over there?' Emily said, nodding at an old man with long, wavy grey hair.

'What would the famous guitarist from Queen and astrophysicist be doing in the Museum Gardens on Bonfire Night? I'm sure he's got better things to do. Like badger watching…'

'Yes, I'm sure you're right,' Emily said, watching the figure disappear into the crowd in front of the museum.

'I'm a victim!' Milton shouted as he was dragged towards the fire. 'A victim… I'm the one who was trying to stop Miles from blowing you all up.'

'He's lying!' Miles shouted at the crowd. 'He's trying to save his skin. He was the one who was going to blow up a bomb and kill and maim you all. That's why he escaped from prison this morning. He is a violent criminal.'

'It's not true,' Milton protested, as he was pulled through the gates of the gardens. 'If anyone was going to blow anyone up, it was him.'

'He's a liar!' Miles shouted.

'Let's just burn them both!' a Guy Fawkes said and the crowd roared in agreement.

'Stop!' Milton cried, as he was pulled towards the pyre.

'Murderer!' a voice called out.

'Burn him!' another shouted.

'Throw them both on the fire!'

Milton gazed out at the masked faces in the crowd. Cows, badgers, Guy Fawkeses and kids in Radiohead T-shirts.

'This is a farce,' he called out. 'A farce!'

More of a tragedy, thought Theodore, trying to get to Milton. But the crowd had a million booted-feet that stomped the ground around him.

Then a combat boot came down on his tail. He let out a yowl. 'That's my tail!' He yowled again.

As the combat boot lifted, he pulled his tail out and beneath his body.

He looked around. He saw a stone stump: the remnant of one of the old columns of St Mary's Abbey. He made for it.

Jonathan and Emily were searching in the shadows of the ruins.

'We're never going to find him,' Jonathan said. 'There are too many people about.'

'I know he's out here somewhere,' Emily said. 'We can't give up on him now.'

'Isn't that Willie Nelson over there?' Jonathan said, pointing at a short man with a ponytail.

'Looks more like Tom Yorke,' Emily said.

'Don't be stupid... What would the lead singer of Radiohead be doing at a protest demonstration in the Museum Gardens on Bonfire Night?'

'I could say the same about Willie Nelson.'

Just then they heard a yowl.

'Did you hear that?' Emily said.

'It sounded like a peacock,' Jonathan said.

'There hasn't been a peacock in the gardens for years,' Emily said. 'It was Theo. He's in trouble... Come on!'

Emily pushed her way through the crowd towards the fire. Jonathan followed.

'I knew nothing about a bomb,' Milton protested as he was dragged towards the fire. He could feel the heat on his face.

'He's guilty,' a Guy Fawkes shouted. 'I found the bomb. It was in a bag by the Roman Column. He had set it to go off and kill us...' He held up the blue rucksack.

'The monster!' a Radiohead fan called out.

'I managed to defuse it,' the Guy Fawkes said. 'Before it exploded.'

'You're a hero,' the Radiohead fan said.

'Burn him! Burn him! Burn him!' the crowd chanted at Milton.

'I never put it there,' Milton protested. 'I wasn't even sure there was a bomb.'

'Of course you did,' Miles cried. 'He planned to kill you all. He phoned me from Full Sutton and said he had plans for this evening. I was trying to stop him. When I found out he had escaped from prison, I knew I had to find him and stop him. Burn him!'

'Burn him! Burn him! Burn him!' the crowd chanted, pushing Milton towards the flames.

Then a flare went off. The ruins of St Mary's Abbey were lit up in blue-white light.

Milton spotted Theodore standing on the stump of an old column.

He pointed at the cat. 'That cat knows the truth,' he cried. 'He knows that I was trying to stop Miles. I wasn't the one who planted the bomb…'

The crowd turned to look at the cat.

Theodore stared out at the masked faces and then at Milton. He knew that whatever he said, it wasn't going to save Milton. He miaowed out Milton's innocence knowing that it would fall on deaf ears.

Then Miles said, 'It's just a big fluffy cat!'

There were loud murmurings among the crowd.

'Maybe it's not just a cat,' a girl in a cow costume said.

Theodore miaowed again.

'It seems to be trying to tell us something,' a badger-faced boy said.

'Let's put it to the test,' a Radiohead fan said. 'Form a space between the cat and these two…'

The crowd parted to create a corridor between the cat and the two brothers.

The Radiohead fan now addressed Theodore. 'Now, let us know which of these brothers is telling the truth. Is it Milton, the escaped murderer? Was he actually trying to stop his brother from setting off a bomb this evening?

'Or was Milton indeed trying to stop his brother, the disgraced banker Miles Macavity, from setting off a bomb in the crowd?'

Theodore stood on the column. He looked from the face of one brother to the other.

'Here kitty, kitty…,' Miles pleaded.

'You remember me, don't you?' Milton said. 'I'm the one who saved you from the river. I'm the one who made a fire and warmed your fur. I'm the one who fed you toasted marshmallows…'

With that, Theodore jumped down and trotted over to Milton. He brushed against his legs.

'The cat says Milton is the good guy,' the badger boy said. 'So Miles must be the bad guy.'

'Then it's Miles that we'll burn on the bonfire,' the cow girl said.

And so Miles was dragged off to be burned on the fire.

'Well, I guess I owe you one,' Milton said to the cat.

Theodore miaowed up at the escaped convict. He narrowed his eyes.

'What's this?' Milton said. 'You want me to give myself in?'

Theodore miaowed again.

'Well, we did stop Miles and that's why I broke out. I guess you've got a point.'

'And I think you should give me back my shirt and jeans,' Jonathan said, pushing his way through to the front of the crowd.

'Well, I did just borrow them from your washing line,' Milton said. 'I'll make sure they're returned as soon as I've handed myself in…'

Then Emily approached Theodore. 'Theo!' she cried.

Theodore raced towards his human and jumped into her arms. As they hugged, more fireworks lit up the sky.

'I'm so glad I've got you back,' Emily said, staring into his big, green eyes. 'Whatever were you thinking: going out on Bonfire Night?'

Then floodlights lit up the whole of the Museum Gardens. Everyone turned towards the light.

'What's going on?' Emily said, clutching Theodore to her chest.

Jonathan noticed a huge banner hanging down the building's façade:

ROCK FOR UNITY!

Then Brian May appeared on the museum roof, his guitar strapped over his shoulder.

'It is Brian May!' Jonathan said.

He was shortly joined by Radiohead singer Tom Yorke.

'It is Tom Yorke!' Emily said.

'No, that's Willie Nelson,' Jonathan said.

The crowd burst into applause.

'And that's Phil Collins on drums!' Jonathan said as a huge drum kit was picked out by a spotlight and Phil did a drumroll to thunderous applause.

I knew there was something in the air tonight, thought Theodore, pushing himself against Emily's chest.

'I didn't know that there was going to be a rock concert,' Jonathan said.

'Me neither,' Emily said.

Brian approached the microphone, set up on the edge of the building. 'Take off your masks!' he called out to the crowd. 'We must unite to be strong. Together we are stronger. Together we can fight the system. Together we can make a difference…

'We must act now for our planet. We must act now for the cows, for the badgers, for the polar bears. Climate change is real. We cannot be complacent. But we must do it together.'

The crowd applauded.

Then Tom Yorke/Willie Nelson joined Brian May at the microphone. 'We must stop hiding behind masks,' he said. 'We must stop fighting amongst ourselves. We must forget our differences… We must work together!'

The crowd cheered.

'Cast off your masks and be yourselves! Now is the time to come together! Together we are stronger!'

People in the crowd began to take off their masks.

'Now burn your masks and outfits!' Brian cried. 'Throw your shackles onto the bonfire!'

Members of the crowd began to approach the bonfire and throw on their masks and costumes. There were whoops and cheers. People began to hug one another.

The cow furry and the badger furry who had been fighting in front of York Minster half an hour earlier took off their fluffy heads and threw them onto the bonfire. They turned and faced each other.

The cow furry smiled at the badger furry. 'Hug?' she said.

The badger furry smiled back. 'Hug,' he said.

They hugged each other and soon they were kissing.

I wonder what their offspring will look like? wondered Theodore. Compact cows with stripy noses and pointed hooves perhaps.

'What's that awful smell?' Emily said, wincing.

'I think it's the smell of burning flesh and plastic,' Jonathan said, his hand across his mouth and nose.

'It stinks,' said Emily.

Theodore miaowed impatiently. Can we please go home now?

Probably the most sensible idea you've had for quite some time, came the voice of the cat basket.

'Yes, come on,' Emily said, looking down at Theodore. 'Let's get Theo home!'

'Yes,' Jonathan said, 'I think a large mug of Yorkshire Tea is in order after the day I've had.'

'After the day *you've* had?'

'After the day *we've* had.'

I think a 12 hour nap is in order, thought Theodore as he was carried through the crowd.

As they approached the gates to the Museum Gardens, the band on the roof of the museum began to blast out The Beatles' *Come Together*.

Theodore glanced down and saw a flyer on the ground, creased and smeared with mud:

ROCK FOR UNITY – 5 NOVEMBER
Super Group Tribute Band!
Featuring…

Brian Maybe-May on guitar

Thom York (without an 'e') on vocals (Radiohead
tribute and Willie Nelson lookalike)
Phil Collings (with a 'g') on drums

Plus Very Special Guests!!!

It wasn't Willie Nelson or Thom Yorke, Theodore
thought disappointedly. Just some copycats…

As they neared home, Theodore heard a voice.
I'm here waiting for you. Come on then!
Theodore realised it was his cat basket calling. He
struggled in Emily's arms.
'I think he knows he's near home,' Jonathan said.
'Yes, I think he does,' Emily said.
She put him down on the pavement.
*Come on then! Your bed is nice and warm and waiting for
you…*
Theodore began to run. He dashed down the side of a
house. He jumped over boundary walls until he reached
his own backyard. He darted through the cat flap into the
kitchen. There in front of him was his cat basket. He
dived inside.
Welcome back, Theo!
By the time Emily and Jonathan unlocked the front
door Theodore was purring from within his fur-lined
cocoon.
'I think he's glad to be home,' Emily said. 'I know I
am.'
'Yes,' Jonathan said. 'I'll put the kettle on.'
'And after a nice cup of Yorkshire Tea, we could have
an early night,' Emily said. 'We don't need to be up in the
morning now my parents are looking after Joseph…'
'Perhaps we could skip the tea?'

Porridge Eaters

'Following a surprise concert in the Museum Gardens in York last night, human remains have been discovered in a bonfire,' the newsreader read. 'The police have stated that they do not suspect foul play. They are not looking for anyone in connection with the incident.'

Jonathan raised an eyebrow, not looking away from the television screen. Well, that's the end of Miles Macavity, he thought.

Theodore peered out from the safety of his cat basket. Well, that's the end of Miles Macavity, he thought.

'In other news: Milton Macavity is back behind bars having given himself in to the police in the early hours of this morning at Fulford Police Station. He said it was a bit cold outside and he got hungry and wanted his porridge.'

'In other local news today, a man has been found in a suitcase on a roundabout in the Tang Hall area of York. A passer-by heard noises and, on opening the suitcase, discovered the man bound and gagged with gaffer tape. The man is being cared for at York Hospital. At present it is not known how he came to be in the suitcase.'

Theodore raised an eyebrow. Yesterday it was a cat in a packed lunch bag; today a man in a suitcase. Was there a connection? he wondered.

Don't start getting involved again in human affairs, came the voice from around him. *You keep your nose out of it.*

Yes, you're probably right, Theodore thought back.

Emily came into the kitchen. 'I wonder if Joseph's had his porridge yet,' she said. 'I should call my mum and make sure he's all right.'

Porridge, thought Theodore. The food of human juveniles, old people with no teeth and prisoners, certainly not fit for feline consumption.

He peered out across the kitchen. He noticed his cat flap set into the door.

Don't even think about it, came the voice of the cat basket. *You stay home and rest…*

Theodore closed his eyes. Yes, I might just stay home and nap today, he thought.

York, November 2016 – November 2019

A Note on the Author

The author lives in York and drinks exclusively
Yorkshire Gold (If anyone from Taylors of Harrogate
reads this little book, donations of tea in return for the
shameless product placement in this book can be sent
to the author, care of the publisher).

Severus House